#1

CELIA SCIENCE
& ANNA ART
The Computer
Code Mystery

## JUSTIN TAYLOR

### ILLUSTRATED BY
### LINDSAY HORNSBY

I_AM SELF-PUBLISHING

@iamselfpub
www.iamselfpublishing.com

# FREE DOWNLOAD

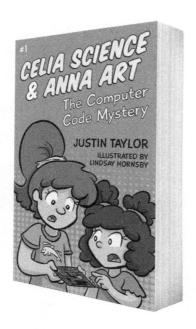

Sign up for the author's New Releases mailing list and to download a FREE copy of this audio book.

Click here to get started:
www.celiascience.com/book1

# CHAPTER 1

Celia rotated the motherboard in her mind, studying each of its thousand connections. She sat stone still on her bed, holding a battered installation manual and a flashlight. Pink light filtered through the fabric, bathing her small bedroom in gentle hues. In her tent, she smelled the summer breeze of the fabric softener that she had grown to equate with 100 percent focused concentration. A soft tap on her shoulder rushed her back through layers of thought and slammed her mind back to her bedroom and the quiet stillness of the winter night.

Mom's face appeared stark in the glare of the flashlight. "Celia, I gave you a five-minute lights-out warning an hour ago."

"Okay, mom, but I think I'm really close to figuring out how to boost the speed of our motherboard."

"Ceil, the last time you said that, it cost me $150 and we had to change all the light bulbs in the office."

Celia blushed as she remembered the sparks and the chaos of that day. "Ummm, a slightly incorrect calculation of the voltage. I forgot to carry the two when I was multiplying. It could happen to anyone."

Her mom gave her a long kiss on top of her head and said, "What am I going to do with you, my little electrical engineer?"

"Keep me," came the reply, muffled by the blanket-tent, followed by the "click" of the flashlight. The room was dark but Celia's mind was alight with visions of motherboards and circuits.

The next morning, Celia opened her eyes and saw snowflakes sticking to her window, just to the right of her bed. The excitement of the possibilities made her heart pound. Could it be, she thought, but she couldn't dare to hope. Too many times, an early morning snow had melted, leaving her to trudge to the bus stop in her over-sized snow boots. On those days, the wind felt extra cold and the day passed with excruciating slowness.

Today felt different, it felt... promising.

Celia shot up from her bed, walked into her dad's office and got on his computer. She went to their local TV station's website and clicked on the snowman's face, which was the "School Closings" link. Sure enough in the middle of the page, she read, "Murrysville – Jefferson Elementary School closed all day". She shut her eyes and said a silent prayer of gratitude. Finally, she would have a day when she could do whatever she wanted.

She felt like she should go back to her bed, snuggle under her blankets and sleep for as long as possible. Almost every morning, she was still tired when her alarm went off. She supposed that was the price she paid for being a night owl. Since she was little, she thought better at night. Her best ideas for inventions came in the still darkness, under her blanket-tent with her sketchpad, flashlight, and multi-colored pen.

She knew that this morning, she could not go back to sleep. She was too excited to be free from school. The music coming from downstairs would have made it impossible to get back to sleep if she tried. Her younger brother and sister, Anna and Silas, were already having a dance party in the living room, celebrating their freedom from the educational overlords.

Celia went downstairs, sat cross-legged on the couch, and watched the big snowflakes fall lazily to the ground. On her lap, she held her snap-in circuit board and the illustrated schematic book she had been studying the night before.

As she held the manual for the computer's inner workings, she felt relaxed. Last night as she slept, the answer came to her. She needed to stack the motherboards. It was that simple. For months, she had tried different ways to jam more circuits flat onto the motherboard. She was at a dead end, until last night.

She dreamed she was Jack and climbed a beanstalk made of computer wires and pieces. All along the way, she saw circuits stacked like pieces of ham, cheese and lettuce inside a sandwich. The higher she climbed, the more stacks of circuits she passed, the faster she traveled. It would work for her too. Stacking the circuits and the motherboards would make the computer run much faster.

That morning as she watched the snow fall, she imagined stacking several motherboards and running a cooling line between them to suck away the heat. It was simple but not easy. Now she needed to figure out how to make it work.

She went to their big storage closet under the stairs and dug out the three old computers Dad intended to take to the electronic recycling service. She removed the motherboards, the wires, and the power packs and carried all of the pieces into her dad's office. Next, she went to the garage and found the old gigantic fish tank, its pump, and the old garden hose.

Finally, she brought her mom the drill and three eight-ounce cans of beans.

"Mom, please drill two half-inch holes in these cans, on the curved sides. I need to use them for their convection."

Mom could tell from the look on Celia's face that she was determined to create her plan.

"Celia," Mom said, "if you are planning on mixing water and electricity, you need an adult to help you. That is super, super dangerous. You could kill yourself."

Celia had not thought of this angle. The "danger element". It did not discourage her; it just gave her pause.

"Good point, Mom," said Celia. "Can you please help me?"

"Not today, sweetie, I have a million things I have to get done. I can help you this weekend," said Mom.

"I can't wait that long, I need to get this done today," said Celia. "Can I start calling relatives until I can find someone who can come over here and help with this?"

"Sure," said Mom, "knock yourself out."

Mom put on her safety glasses, took the cans outside and drilled two holes in each. The beans quickly drained from the cans. They were sacrificed for science. By the time Mom was putting up the drill and cleaning the beans off the drill bit, Grandma pulled up in the driveway. She entered the house wearing a big smile.

"How are my grandkids this morning?"

Anna and Silas stopped dancing and ran downstairs to Grandma's open arms. "Grandma! Grandma!" Lots of hugs and kisses were exchanged. After that, Grandma bounded up the basement steps to the kitchen. Celia was waiting for her and said, "Grandma, we have a tough engineering challenge today. We are building a water cooling loop for a set of motherboards."

"Piece of cake," said Grandma, "I can build one of these in my sleep."

Celia knew she could. Grandma and Mom both had a way of figuring out anything mechanical. Grandma gave Celia's mom a big hug. Celia's mom said, "Thanks for coming over, Mom. She needs some adult supervision with this since she is mixing water and electricity. And I just don't have time to help her today."

"Happy to help," said Grandma. "Anything for my Celia." Then she and Celia walked into the office and shut the door.

In Celia's past experience, ideas seemed straight forward until she began to make them real. Only then did the challenges begin. The hard work was always in the details of motherboard design and hacking. Thinking of the concept was fun; implementing it required focus and diligence.

While her brother and sister jumped up and down and spun around to the wild music pulsing from the speakers, Celia and Grandma had the office door shut and hardly noticed the noise. They were diligently planning their day of electrical and hydro engineering.

Celia came out of the room a few times. She had to get black electrical tape and silicone caulk from the garage. Around noon to 2p.m., they spent a couple of hours testing something in the bathroom. Shortly after that, they quickly ate cheese sandwiches for lunch. Eventually, Celia and Grandma took a plastic mat outside along with the fish tank.

By that evening, Celia and Anna were playing on the newly-improved computer. Each of the motherboards was wired together and sitting on a separate shelf of the wooden bookcase. The main black computer case sat on top of the bookshelf. All of the wires linking the extra motherboards to the main motherboard had been cut, spliced and wrapped in electrical tape to extend them so they would span to the primary motherboard.

Water whirled as it flowed through the old garden hose and circulated around the room. Each motherboard had a bean can taped to it, directly on top of the processor. The cans acted as water reservoirs and heat sinks, pulling heat away from the processors. Each can had one piece of hose going in, and a different piece of hose going out. The space around the hole where the hose went into the can was sealed with silicone caulk and wrapped with electrical tape.

The last hose dropped out through the cracked window and into the fish tank outside on the rubber mat sitting on the ground. Warm water poured into the tank after it had circulated across all the boards. A separate hose was attached to the old fish tank pump and ran the water back up into the circulating system.

As a finishing touch, Celia even put her little goldfish "Bobby" into the tank. The water warmed by the computer kept his tank at a nice temperature, as long as the machine ran at full power and all the processors were putting off a lot of heat. For good measure, Celia had every fan in the house in her dad's office. Despite all of that, the boards still radiated enough heat to fill the small office.

The collection of motherboards was much hotter than Celia had expected. But her calculations had been correct about one thing, the new configuration was fast. It was insanely powerful to the point that it was almost unbelievable. Celia and Anna were playing the Mermaid Power! game online and there were 200 other people playing with them. The speed of their mermaid was jaw dropping. Their mermaid was like a pink bolt of lightning, zooming around the ocean. She was swimming circles around all of the other players!

As the girls laughed and talked about the mermaid, the picture on the screen became fuzzy then returned to normal. Then it became even fuzzier, and it again adjusted to normal.

Suddenly, the game disappeared. Numbers and letters flashed quickly in lines filling the screen. The girls moved the arrow keys and the mouse but nothing happened.

"Celia! What did you do to the game!?! You broke it, now the computer is doing crazy things!" Anna said.

"I didn't break it. That looks like some kind of code," Celia responded.

Thinking quickly, Celia grabbed the phone on her dad's desk and shot a video of the letters and numbers flying across the screen. They seemed to move like waves, a ripple of vowels, a surge of prime numbers, a group of lines with real words, then back to randomness. Celia took three minutes of video, which completely filled the phone's memory. After that, the letters and numbers kept going for another two minutes.

Anna ran through the house to get Mom. By the time she and Mom returned, the code had disappeared. When Mom saw the video, she was not pleased.

"Ah, Ceil, that is a virus! You opened up the computer to hackers with your crazy experiments, now all of our files are probably destroyed," Celia's mom complained.

"Mom, I don't think it is a virus, I think it is a code. Someone somewhere is trying to send messages that can only be read by superfast computers talking to each other through the Mermaid Power! game site," explained Celia.

"Who in the world would do that?" said Mom.

"Who indeed?" said Anna.

# CHAPTER 2

She sat alone in the room, quiet except for the clicks and squeals of her pets. She called them her mermaids, but they were really dolphins with fake mermaid tails. The tails were itchy and irritated the dolphins' skin, but Rachel Stone did not care about the discomfort she caused the dolphins.

There were only three things in the world Rachel Stone did care about:

1) Having the all-time super, awesomest, unbeatable score on her favorite multi-player game, Mermaid Power!

2) Thinking of new ways to write computer programs for evil purposes, and

3) Money.

She thought about these three things almost every second of the day. Sometimes, she thought about what it would be like to be a real mermaid and be able to live underwater and talk to fish. But eventually, those thoughts turned into ideas about writing evil computer programs or making money, and the vicious cycle continued.

The dolphins' tank was in the middle of her sprawling command room. The right wall was full of screens; the top of the dolphins' tank was a 20-foot diameter circular hole in the middle of the floor, on the left was an L-shaped desk with three screens, two keyboards and one chair that could spin around in every direction. This room was huge and the far wall had solid windows, looking out onto the blue expanse of the Pacific Ocean. In the far right corner between the wall of screens and the wall of windows was a single computer with a pink case, and a small desk. In front of this computer was a chair, covered in purple crushed velvet, and its armrests had mermaids carved into them. This was Rachel's favorite computer; all she did on it was play Mermaid Power!

From their spot in the middle of the room, the dolphins did all they could to let Rachel know how they felt about her. They spoke to her only in deep, angry clicks. They spit water at her when she came near their tank. They would have done more, had they been equipped with useful things, like hands or hula-hoops or LASERS.

Rachel Stone was 25 years old. She was born in Pomona, California, near Los Angeles. From an early age, people noticed she had an unusually bright and focused mind. Her mom and dad could not afford a computer when she was a child, so she became a middle school volunteer at her local library. She soon began to spend all of her time there in its small media center, working on the computers. While most people came and went from the room after researching a topic or two, Rachel stayed for hours. The content on the internet did not fascinate her as much as learning all about how the internet worked.

When she was in sixth grade, she took a bus across town to the campus of the California Institute of Technology (Caltech) to attend a lecture by Dr Elizabeth Washington from the Center for Applied and Computational Mathematics. Before the lecture, Rachel printed and studied Dr Washington's last 12 published papers. She found the lecture hall and arrived in the room 20 minutes early, sitting in the middle of the first row. She had a notebook with each of her top fifty questions neatly printed, allowing five lines between them to take notes on the responses.

For the next 20 minutes, students filled the room; by the time Dr Washington entered and came to the podium, the room was 25 percent full. Most of the undergraduates in attendance were there only to earn extra credit in their computational mathematics classes. To take attendance, Dr Washington put her email address on the board at the front of the room and asked the students to email her so she could collect a list of attendees.

For the next hour, Dr Washington talked in detail about the latest article she had published in the prestigious Journal of Scientific and Statistical Computing. Rachel was familiar with the article and had read it in detail three nights ago, carefully highlighting interesting passages and writing questions in her notebook so she could remember to ask Dr Washington. Rachel was the only one who had done this. In a stark contrast to Rachel, the undergraduates in attendance seemed bored to the point of agony. One could feel all of their eyes staring at the clock so hard, it seemed they would burn the numbers off its face.

At the end of her lecture, Dr Washington opened the floor for questions. One small hand went up in the room filled with some of the brightest young minds in the world. Dr Washington called on the kid in the front row and expected to hear a foreign accent on her English. Caltech regularly attracted a child prodigy or two from around the world, so it was not completely out of the norm to see a 12 year old on campus.

Rachel spoke English with the clear, plain accent of Southern California. This surprised Dr Washington, but not as much as the young girl's question. Rachel's tone seemed desperate, as if she needed her question answered so she could put her mind at ease.

"Dr. Washington, in the abstract to your article, you say there are 'interrelated approaches to support multiple access paths to each terminal object in information hierarchies', and you give the examples of 'faceted classification, faceted search, and coded web directories'. However, in your paper, you only clearly explain faceted classification and virtually ignore faceted search and coded web directories. Even when you provide the formula for faceted search and you insert the set, V1, you only vaguely explain how we can derive V1. Did I miss something?"

Dr Washington was dumbfounded. She had never thought of the equation in that way. The young person in the front row clearly had a mind capable of a different type of thinking.

To Rachel, it felt like a hundred years since the night she first met Dr Elizabeth Washington. In fact, it had been less than 14 years, but her life had changed drastically. Since then, she had learned enough about computers to use them to create hundreds of ways to steal money from thousands of people and businesses. Now she had enough money so that she could buy anything she wanted. But even with all that money, she was not happy. Something was missing from her life; she just did not know what.

This morning, Rachel sat in the front right corner of her spacious command room. She leaned back in her purple chair and rubbed her hands over the soft crushed velvet of its armrests. She stared at the screen while playing her favorite online game, Mermaid Power! She could not believe what she was seeing. At first, her morning game seemed to be going like it usually did. She saw a screen full of mermaids swimming around, making friends, collecting coins, planting seaweed, doing all the things that normal mermaids do. Then she saw one mermaid, a very annoying, maybe insane, mermaid, swimming around so fast that she looked like a blur.

This little pink mermaid collected all the coins from the shipwrecks before Rachel's mermaid even got to the ship. In the time it took Rachel's mermaid to plant one plant, this other mermaid completed an entire garden and got the "double your flippers" bonus!

Rachel sat dumbfounded as she watched the pink mermaid's score climb higher and higher. First 100,000 points, then 200,000, inching towards her own unattainable score, on the top left of the screen. 1,582,963 points... one million, five hundred and eighty- two thousand, nine hundred and sixty-three. That score was her proudest accomplishment. It was the all-time Mermaid Power! high score. She thought it would stand forever, as long as merpeople swam the ocean blue. But this new upstart was thrashing her score like it was vegetables in a blender. Rachel was beginning to feel embarrassed. Her pride felt like a lumpy blob of carrot mush that was shredded to a pulp. The shock of being beaten – or of anyone even coming close – was too much for her to take. She did not like to lose.

She was sure the other player was cheating, but that didn't bother her. Rachel cheated all the time, at everything. Even when she was playing cards with herself, in a game called solitaire, she still cheated. And the only person she beat was herself. Rachel was fine with cheating, as long as she was the one who won and everyone else lost. She could not let this annoying mermaid get any closer to her high score. She had to take action. She would do what she did best... she wrote computer code, and she cheated.

Rachel walked across the room, past her angry dolphins, to her L-shaped desk, where she controlled an incredible amount of computing power. She sat down and had soon cracked the password protecting the Mermaid Power! game site. She then located the player who was superfast. She used a mapping program to get the player's computer address, called an IP address, and discovered her location.

She wanted to slow the player down, so she sent a wave of data, random letters and numbers, into the other player's computer. She wanted to overwhelm the speed of the other player's internet connection. She wanted the turbo-charged mermaid to move more slowly, like a normal mermaid.

After a few minutes, the new player left the game. Rachel's plan had worked perfectly, except for one small mistake that went unnoticed at the time. Instead of sending a random collection of data to slow down the other player's mermaid, she accidentally sent the ultra-top-secret program she was using to steal money from state tax returns.

Later that night, after a full day of writing evil computer codes and dreaming of becoming a mermaid, Rachel was sound asleep. Suddenly she shot up in bed. Something in her dream made her realize what she had done.

"I sent my ultra-top-secret computer code to that girl to slow down her computer. How could I be so careless?" She smacked her forehead with the palm of her hand. Then she took a deep breath. "There's no way the kid who was playing that game has any idea what I sent her. I'm sure she and her family think it was just a crazy computer virus."

Rachel did not know that across the country, in a small house in a suburb near Pittsburgh, one girl was intently studying the three-minute video of letters and numbers flashing across a screen. Celia had turned her mind to solving a puzzle, and she always succeeded.

........
........

It was past 10p.m. Celia lay under her cover, as usual, her flashlight was on, and she had her pad and her multi-colored pen. She had studied the video for two hours straight until the phone battery died.

Mom made Celia plug it in and "give it a rest", as she said. However, during the times Celia watched the video, she became more and more convinced that it was not a random string of data. She knew it was computer code. She saw lines containing DNS (Domain Name System) numbers, redirecting users to a hidden site.

```
sendLink("192.168.154.22")
redirect("192.168.98.16");
```

Those were like big neon signs flashing "something tricky is going on here". After those DNS numbers, Celia slowed down the video and watched it frame by frame. This is what she saw:

```
var number = 0;
LoopWhile (number < 100000000000000) {
    //somecode
    number++;
}
createCrossSiteRequestForgeryLink();
sendLink("192.168.154.22")
redirect("192.168.98.16");
enableRemoteKeylogger();
//capture user and password:
$.ajax({
    type: "POST",
    IP: "192.168.98.16/newAccount/id",
     data: { "account": actNumber, "password":
password },
    dataType: "json",
```

```
success: function( data, textStatus, jqXHR)
   updateRecord(actNumber, password);
})
```

Then the video got blurry as her hand moved while she was filming. She was not sure what that code was for, but she knew how to get started tracking it down. It was too late to get onto the family computer right now, so it would have to wait until tomorrow. All she needed was another snow day.

Her mind was still spinning when she felt the familiar tap of her mom's finger on her shoulder.

"Sweet pea, are you still awake?" her mom whispered.

"Did you guess because of my flashlight and the sound of my pen scratching the paper?" responded Celia.

"Those were good clues," said Mom, "What are you working on?"

Celia peeled back the blanket-tent, looked at her mom and said, "You know what I'm working on."

"Ahhh, the mystery of the computer virus that attacked you during the Mermaid Power! play-a-thon this afternoon?" Mom said. "Of course! I know you gathered a lot of clues as you drained the phone battery. I suggest you close your eyes and let all the clues float around in your brain as you try to go to sleep. A lot of times, you can't reach an answer when you think about it directly. You need to let your mind be free and think of other things, bunny rabbits, marshmallows and—"

"Ada Lovelace!" Celia interjected. She liked to say the name of her favorite scientist whenever she got a chance.

"Yes," her mom said sweetly, "and Ada Lovelace, if that helps your mind relax and lets you get some rest. It's not good to stay up so late every night, you need your sleep. Sleep is what allows your body to flush the free radicals from your brain."

"Mom, I'm not even going to ask what that means."

"Oh nothing, Ceil, you will learn about it someday. Off with the flashlight and to the land of dreams and Ada Lovelace with you," Mom said.

With that, she walked out of the room. Ten minutes later, Celia was sound asleep, dreaming of mermaids and computer programs.

# CHAPTER 3

The next morning, Celia again woke up on her own, a good sign. Again, she saw more snow on her window, an even better sign. She looked over at her clock; it said 9:42. Hallelujah, she thought joyfully, that confirms it, I don't even have to check the internet, NO SCHOOL AGAIN!!!! HOOOORAY!!! The excitement filled her body so much that a little shiver of energy passed through her.

As Celia's feet hit the floor, she saw the best surprise of all; her dad was back from his business trip! He came across the room, scooped her up and gave her lots of good kisses on her head and cheeks. She squeezed him as tightly as she could.

"Dad, I'm so glad you are back, I've been working on a real puzzle," Celia said.

"Lucky for us, you don't have school today; we should have plenty of time to work on this strange puzzle you have uncovered."

Celia liked that her dad usually believed her off-the-wall ideas about conspiracies and potential schemes. She also liked that he was very good at researching things on the internet, when he wasn't busy working on things for his job.

"Don't you have to work in your office today?"

"Yes I do," he said, "but since someone helped to double the speed of my computer, I can get all my work done in half

25

the time. I can start a little bit later today; I haven't seen you all week. I missed you."

They walked to the kitchen and Dad poured another cup of coffee. Then he made Celia two lightly toasted pieces of bread, smeared with peanut butter and honey. "Brain food", he called it.

"Okay, kid, show me what you got."

Celia grabbed the phone from its charger and showed her dad the video of the strange numbers and letters flashing across the screen. She zoomed in and paused it to show him the things she thought were lines of computer code. She explained to her dad how the resolution got fuzzy before the numbers and letters flooded the screen.

"Very interesting," her dad said in a German-sounding scientific voice. "Vee vill need to investigate furder, but first, VEE SHOVEL!"

Until this time, Anna and Silas were in the living room playing Mind Control – a game where they sat two feet apart and looked at each other. They took turns trying to guess what the other one was thinking. Somehow, it seemed that Silas always thought Anna was thinking about "doggies" or "num-nums". At once, when they heard Dad say, "VEE SHOVEL!", they both jumped up and ran into the kitchen and began to shout-sing:

"SHO-VEL! SHO-VEL! SHO-VEL!"

Dad jumped up and started to dance as he sang, "Shovel, shovel, shovel."

Anna and Silas started to sing as well. "Shovel dance, shovel dance, shovel dance, WOO!!"

"Scoop, scooooop, scoop, OUT, OUT!" sang Silas.

Everyone put on their hats, jackets, boots and gloves, and then headed outside to shovel the snow. It had been snowing almost every other day for the last three weeks, so the snow was piled high along their driveway.

Celia's two-year-old brother, Silas, was the most enthusiastic shoveler, and shouted with joy the entire time he worked, though he did not really move much snow off the driveway.

Dad, Celia and Anna worked like a tight team and had the driveway completely clean within 20 minutes.

Next, they all picked up their shovels and walked without a word to the driveway of their elderly neighbors, Roger and Cindy. They spent the next 30 minutes shoveling that driveway and then sweeping it with a big janitor broom to get the last of the snow off.

Celia loved to shovel snow. It was the perfect task for letting her brain think in an organized and thorough way. Her hands and legs were busy, blood pumping, out in the crisp, fresh air of the winter. Her mind was free to think about anything it wanted, since the physical task didn't require much thinking.

She began to develop a plan of how she could figure out what was going on with the code. She was developing a hypothesis. Now she just needed to test it.

When they finished shoveling, they were all pretty tired. They felt proud because their hard work had paid off, with two clean driveways.

They took off their wet boots and gloves downstairs and then went upstairs to the kitchen. They found that Mom had four mugs of hot cocoa waiting for them. They all sat in the kitchen for a few minutes and listened to the news on the radio. The weatherman predicted another six inches of snow that afternoon!

"Well, sounds like we will need to do more shoveling later, so rest up," said Dad.

Eventually, everyone left the kitchen. Anna went to her room to work on an art project. She was creating a scene of downtown Murrysville, complete with shops and figures. Silas went to the basement to play with his trucks, dogs, and dinosaurs, and to create a big, imaginary world that would keep him busy five minutes at a time, until a major problem caused him to need someone, usually mommy. He would shout, "Hooop, hooop, Mommy hooop!" until she came downstairs to see what was the matter. This continued in five-minute cycles until lunchtime. Celia took her hot cocoa to the office to test her hypothesis.

Celia's dad was in his office on the big computer, working for his job. He always had many lines of numbers and equations on his screen, and he was on the phone a lot. Most of the time he drank coffee and didn't talk much; instead, he listened attentively through his earpiece. His job seemed very strange and confusing to Celia. She thought of work as a place that you went to do things. Or time you spent out in the world learning things, like a scientist, or a mechanic working on cars. For that kind of work, you could see what you were working towards; with her dad's job, she couldn't really tell what he was working towards.

Since he was using the big computer in his office, she borrowed her mom's laptop and took it to her room, then she cleared away the bits of rock and seashell from her desk. She sat down at the desk and opened up the laptop. The first thing she wanted to do was to try to replicate the results from the previous day. She went to the Mermaid Power! website, signed in, and began to play. Since she was not on the super-powered computer in the office, her mermaid did not travel at lightning-fast speed, but it was still really fun to play the game, and she played for over an hour.

Slowly, Celia realized that the letters and numbers were not going to appear on the screen like they had the day before. So she moved to plan "B", which was to figure out what kind of computer code was flashing on the screen.

Celia got her notebook and began to search the phrases of code she had copied down from the screen. She learned that the code was from a computer language called JavaScript, which was used to group together actions that run on the internet. Interestingly, most of the code was a series of custom functions that had been named to tell what they did.

```
var number = 0;
LoopWhile (number < 100000000000000) {
  //somecode
  number++;
}
```

This was some kind of looping function that took the code below it and ran it over and over the number of times shown in the parameter.

```
sendLink("192.168.154.22")
redirect("192.168.98.16");
```

These were likely two functions to take a user from a site where they thought they were going to an entirely different location on the internet. The long number to the right is a DNS number, which logs the location of everything on the internet and points computers to the correct servers.

Since the DNS numbers are inside the (), Celia knew they were parameters for the function. Something inside the function "redirect" told it that it needed the information inside the () to know where to go.

```
enableRemoteKeylogger();
```

The function enableRemoteKeylogger seemed like a function that would capture the information typed by a user and log it remotely somewhere else. It was probably to collect passwords.

```
//capture user and password:
```

The // shows that this is a comment inserted by the coder. It says exactly what the function above does. It captures the username and password.

```
$.ajax({
  type: "POST",
  dns: "192.168.98.16/newAccount/id",
   data: { "account": actNumber, "password":
password },
```

This function is an AJAX function, which is a big, flashing neon sign saying, "sending data, sending data". From the functions, it looks like they are sending account numbers and passwords.

Next, she typed the website that was in the code: www.statetax.gov. Since it was a website that ended in .gov, it was probably a government site. And since the name of it was state tax, it probably had to do with taxes. Why was someone writing a computer program in the Mermaid Power! game about taxes? That did not make any sense.

Or did it?

# CHAPTER 4

After eight straight hours on her mom's laptop, Celia left her bedroom. She walked downstairs in a daze. She slid onto the couch in the living room, opposite to the big window that looked out onto the street. The sun was down; night comes early in the middle of winter in Pennsylvania. The porch light across the street lit dots of snow as they drifted down, swirling in the restless mountain wind, creating a glare on the surface of the quiet street.

Her head hurt from learning so much new information. Her eyes ached from looking at the screen so closely and for such a long time. Her wrists and shoulders were stiff from holding them still, as she slowly learned to create new JavaScript code.

When she sat down in front of her mom's laptop, she did not plan to learn JavaScript. She began to search the bits of code she picked out from the jumble of letters and numbers on the video. As she searched, she kept seeing advertisements for free online computer language coding lessons. She decided to try lesson one from code.org.

During her first lesson in JavaScript, she wrote code that turned the cursor into a smiley face. That was all it took. She was hooked. Eight hours later, she was on lesson four. She still could not figure out all of the commands in the code she recorded referring to Statetax.gov. She knew it did have encryption-destroying scripts, embedded as a separate

JUSTIN TAYLOR

batch of events. That meant that someone was trying to hack passwords and break into places where they should not be. It also meant they were likely trying to steal tax money.

This was some kind of looping function that took the code below it and ran it over and over the number of times shown in the parameter.

She also knew that the creator of the code was way beyond lesson four of the code.org website.

Anna came into the room. "What'cha up to, Celia?" she asked.

Celia did not hear her; she was not listening or seeing, she was just sitting. She was letting the whole world swirl around her and do what it wanted. She wasn't asleep, her eyes were open, but she was not paying any attention to what was happening around her. All she was thinking about was the JavaScript code. Specifically, the program she just wrote that directed a little, cute puppy around the screen as you clicked it with your mouse. The person who attacked me could write that puppy code in their sleep, thought Celia. How am I ever going to figure out who it was? How, how, how...

She let that question linger in her mind until it scattered like ashes blowing in the wind.

Since they hadn't had school for two days, and Dad was home early from his business trip, they had one of their family's favorite meals – BREAKFAST FOR DINNER!!! The tempting smells of cooking pancakes pulled Celia out of the code-induced stupor. Mom made her special super-fluffy pancake

34

batter, and Dad cooked them on the skillet. While he cooked the pancakes, he also made a big cheese and veggie omelet to go with it. He always made a big show of using both hands to flip his giant omelet in the air and catch it back in the pan.

"I've still got it," he would say.

Mom even found the last quart bag of last summer's blueberries in the garage freezer. The small bag of purple and black treasures was from an afternoon in early July when Celia and Anna helped grandma pick and freeze them. Dad used them to make sweet and tart blueberry compote in a small saucepan on the stove. Anna stood on a little stool at the corner of the stove, stirring the compote and telling stories of picking berries with Grandma and Celia. The smell of blueberries filled the house, making everyone's mouths water and bringing back memories of walking barefoot in Grandma's backyard on warm July days.

"If we only had some fresh mint," said Dad, "that would really make this compote pop!" Dad loved to watch cooking shows and was always talking about different foods "POPPING", or something "completing a dish". Celia and Anna thought it was funny when Dad talked like that about the food he was cooking at home.

When dinner was announced, Celia came to the table and saw something truly beautiful. Her plate was piled with fluffy pancakes, topped with creamy butter, blueberry compote and real maple syrup. Beside them rested a slice of perfectly-cooked omelet, cheese oozing out the sides, tiny bits of red pepper, mushroom, and caramelized onion peeking out in colorful bursts from the yellow of the egg. She almost cried with joy.

After her first bite, she was in heaven. The best part was the blueberry compote, mixed with the melted butter. It tasted just like the July afternoon when she had helped her grandma pick, wash and freeze 72 pints of blueberries. It was so much work, but now she knew that it had all been worth it to bring a little bit of summer to the frigid Pennsylvania winter.

Celia ate slowly, enjoying every bite. Silas had been the first one at the table. He wore only his diaper and said, "Pease, pease" for 20 minutes before dinner, holding up his empty plate to anyone who would listen. When his food finally arrived, he did not even wait for the family to say a blessing. He tore into his food like he hadn't eaten in three days, even though he had eaten an apple just two hours before. He devoured his slice of omelet with greedy handfuls, bits of egg and cheese plastered his chest, shoulder, and even his left earlobe. He looked like a little boy who had gotten into a fight with a cheese omelet, and it was hard to say who won the battle.

Dad commented that he would help Silas eat but he was afraid he would lose a hand if he stuck it near Silas's plate.

Anna neither ate extremely slowly like Celia, nor did she eat like she had never seen food before, the way Silas did. Instead, she ate at a speed somewhere in the middle. She complimented her mom and dad on how yummy the food was, and she never talked with her mouth full. Maybe best of all, she was great at keeping the conversation going at dinner. This was not an easy thing to do when one of the people at the table barely says more than, "Pease, scoop, booboo, doggie," and "Mama".

"So Celia, how did it go today, trying out your new hypothesis for the problem you are working on?" asked Anna.

At first, Celia did not say anything. She was too interested in her pancakes to notice that anyone had spoken. She was enjoying everything about them – not only the smell and taste, but the way they felt when she cut them, and the soft, squishy noise they made. They were perfect.

Anna patiently asked again, "Celia, did you hear me?"

She waited until Celia looked up and their eyes met. She repeated, "So Celia, how did it go today, trying out your new hypothesis for the puzzle you are working on?"

"It was tough, sis. I can't figure out what the code is doing. It has parts that are trying to break secrets, and it has a probe that attempts to go into state tax websites. I can tell that it is trying to do something bad, but I don't know what."

"I heard something on the news about identity theft," Anna responded. "I think it is a thing where bad people try to dress up like other people and steal money from their bank. But, it might be a scheme where people take a telephone number and make long-distance calls, like to Japan and England."

"Really, I wonder if this code has to do with identity theft," pondered Celia.

Her mom and dad looked at each other.

Mom said, "Celia, we know how much fun you have learning about new things and trying to figure out problems, but this one is not what you think it is. A JavaScript computer code did not slip into your Mermaid Power! video game. It was just a random virus that attacked our computer and our anti-virus program took care of it. End of story. That is why you could not replicate it today when you tried to play it again on my laptop." Mom continued, "There is nothing to replicate, it was a random, crazy thing that happened. It was just a coincidence that you were playing Mermaid Power! when the craziness impacted the computer. So just forget about it. Start trying to take apart a different mystery. There are lots of unexplained things out in the world for you to work on. Just pick something else."

Celia felt a flash of embarrassment come over her and make her face hot. She knew Mom was wrong. She couldn't just forget about it, she knew there was something more to that code. If her parents were not going to help her figure out what was going on, she would have to do it all herself.

........
........

From that day on, Celia was officially obsessed with learning JavaScript. When her family went on their weekly trip to the Murrysville community library, she spent a good bit of time on the library computer, looking at programing books, and she settled on two: "JavaScript programming for beginners" and "JavaScript: a coder's encyclopedia".

"JavaScript programming for beginners" was only 250 pages. It laid out the basic framework for the best way to write a functioning JavaScript program. A DVD came with the book and had lots of great examples. Since every internet browser can run JavaScript, Celia was able to work on the examples exactly like they were shown in the book. It even came with a nice JavaScript Editor that highlights and colors the special JavaScript commands and made learning easier. In the first week, Celia worked all the way through the book twice, including the completion of each of the "additional practice" exercises both times.

The thicker book, "JavaScript: a coder's encyclopedia", was much more difficult to understand. It was basically the definition of each of the different commands in JavaScript. It was almost impossible to get through from start to finish, but Celia did her best.

Just as her obsession with JavaScript was beginning, Celia spent a Saturday helping her grandma at the This-n-That sale at church. When Celia arrived, the church's gym was already packed with an amazing collection of random things. There were couches beside old clothes, and nice tables beside stuffed animals. It was a truly strange assortment of the cast-off belongings from middle-class America.

Celia's job that day was to stick prices on new things as they came in. She also helped customers carry small things to their cars when they had their hands too full to carry any more. Celia was busy all day running in and out of the building, loading cars and unloading possessions. When she wasn't doing that, she was sticking prices on things with the pricing gun. She also pretended she was much older, as she listened to her grandma and her grandma's friends talk about the world.

Soon after she got there, she saw the sale was a goldmine for used computer equipment. As the day continued, she noticed there was a growing pile of computer equipment marked "Does not work, FREE". Celia's mind lit up. This was a rare opportunity, and she was going to take advantage of it.

She spent her spare moments throughout the day picking through the bits and pieces from hundreds of computers. Since they did not work anymore, people thought were worthless, but she knew better. Celia borrowed a small screwdriver from the church maintenance man. She used it to take apart the machines. By the end of the day, she had collected most of the parts needed to build a really, really nice computer. Those parts were:

A computer case: The entire machine is assembled inside of this box. Celia found one with clear plastic side windows. It also had lots of holes, fans, and a dust screen to let air circulate throughout. Besides this, it was big, very big. It was large enough to include several hard drives and two motherboards. The two-motherboard strategy was key to the design she had in mind.

Two motherboards: Each motherboard had the same basic circuit configuration. She planned on using the stacked circuit design that she first used with her dad's computer.

Two custom fans: The fans were key to allowing air to move freely throughout the inside of the machine.

One SSD internal drive: Instead of the spinning drives most computers have, these are digital and more like the additional storage cards used in cell phones and digital cameras. Celia found one in a clean computer that was only a couple of years old. She needed this drive as a backup for the much nicer SCSI internal drive she planned on buying new.

One monitor: Every computer needs a monitor so you can see what is happening. Celia chose one that was small so that it would fit on her desk.

A power pack: She found a power pack from an old server. Since it powered an industrial computer, it might have enough juice to power the configuration she planned to assemble. Celia would have to calculate the power requirements to check if it would work or not.

Eight chips of RAM: RAM is the quick memory that allows each computer to function. Every computer she took apart had RAM on its motherboard. As she took apart each machine, she made stacks of the different kinds of RAM she found. Once she was done, she picked through the stacks. She found the eight best RAM chips and put them in a plastic bag. She took two extras, just in case any of her top eight did not work.

Late in the afternoon, Celia's grandma took her home and she carried all of her treasures in two plastic grocery bags. Celia's grandma carried the computer case and monitor for her. At home, Celia carefully laid out all the pieces on her bed. Her dad came into her room to see how her day had been. He saw the computer parts and understood part of her master plan.

"Celia, if you can tell me which parts of your rig you are missing, I will go online and order them right now. If you don't understand what you have then I won't buy the missing pieces for you. You will have to come back to me later with the right answer."

Immediately, Celia said, "Dad, I need four new quad core processors, a thousand terabyte SCSI hard drive, a sub-zero liquid cooling chill tower, and an EPS 12 Volt, 1,200 watt power supply."

"Ohhhh, sorry, Celia," said Dad, "you don't need a power supply, you already have one." He reached onto the bed and picked up the heavy hunk of metal and plastic.

"Wrong," said Celia, "that power supply you are holding is only 600 watts. I plan on running two boards with two processors each. I need at least 1,200 watts to keep the rig I am building supplied with juice. I will install the 600 watt power supply I have for any surge times when my computer needs more than 1,200 watts."

Her dad shook his head. "What kind of monster are you planning on building? Why would your computer ever need more than 1,200 watts of power? Are you planning on running anti-encryption programs? Actually, I don't even want to know what you are planning."

Celia just smiled and shook her head; Dad was not too far away from guessing her plan.

He continued, "I thought I might be able to trick you. But no, I should have known better. You are absolutely right about what you need. You are even close on calculating how much electricity your new computer will pull, once all the pieces are installed and running at full speed. Great job using your math skills on that one. I guess I need to get on the internet and find the pieces you are looking for, don't I?"

"Dad, you are awesome. Even if you are a terrible dancer," Celia said with a smile.

"Hey! I'm not a terrible dancer! You are awesome too, Ceil."

Dad did an awkward, weird dad-dance as he left her room and went into his office to look for the computer parts on the internet.

········
········

Over the next few days, boxes began to arrive from faraway places. The processors came from Taiwan. The mega-strong power supply came from Germany. The sub-zero cooling tower came from Brazil. The last to arrive was the hard drive from northern California.

As each piece came, it felt like Christmas, as Celia opened up the box and carefully inspected the components. She knew that you can't tell if a computer part will work properly just by looking at the outside of the box, or even at the outside of a component. The only way to know for sure is to assemble the whole thing, plug it in, turn it on, and hope it works. Her dad liked to say, "Building a computer is 90 percent knowledge and 10 percent magic." For Celia, those percentages felt about right for most things in life.

# CHAPTER 5

**T**he next Saturday, Celia put the 90-10 rule to the test over and over. She, along with her Uncle Greg, Aunt BB, Anna, and Mom, built the computer on the dining room table. Dad took Silas sledding so that he would not be in the house causing mischief while everyone else was building the computer. The delicate computer components were spread out on the dining room table, like some kind of crazy Thanksgiving feast for robots. The team was working furiously to construct something that actually worked.

It was a day to remember at the Mason house; lots of testing the correct plug-ins, looking at schematic drawings, and watching instructional videos on the internet. Eventually, after several unsuccessful tries, they turned on the power switch, and the whole computer lit up. Both motherboards lit up, the lights on the boards, the disks spun and whirled inside the hard drives, the fans on the front and sides of the computer, everything just... well, it all just worked.

Celia's mood had gone from hopeful, to nervous, to completely defeated throughout the day. Only Anna remained positive the whole time.

"Don't worry, sis, we have a lot of smart people here, trying to get this thing to work. Plus, we have like 9,000 instructional videos on YouTube we can watch to explain every detail about how to install these components. It will be fine."

After they got the computer to work, Celia knew the really tricky part was up to her. No one in her family could help her do what she needed to accomplish next. She was going to use JavaScript to weave the pieces of hardware together and make her Frankenstein computer something special.

········
········

Eventually, the snow quit falling and the sisters went back to school. This was good news for Anna, since she is a very social person and was getting bored of just hanging out with her family and building snowmen in the backyard. For Celia, however, it was a real drag. She wished she could stay home every day for a month. Then she could play outside a little and read the hardware instruction books that came with her new computer parts. She would have more time to work with the JavaScript programs online to try to figure out how to make her computer as fast as it could be.

The funny thing was that she had not thought about that strange code in weeks. Originally, it was the reason that she began to learn JavaScript, but now, she barely even remembered why she was so worried about it. She didn't think of it again until she decided to play Mermaid Power! on her new Frankenstein computer.

........
........

Celia came home from a rough day at school. It was harder and harder for her to find anyone in fifth grade to talk to, since all she thought about was her computer and creating new programs in JavaScript. Everything she did in school was boring. She could not concentrate on history or spelling. She was also bored in reading class, even though she loved to read. But the crazy fiction books full of silly characters she enjoyed most were pretty far away from the works she had to read for class.

She found herself alone in her room, looking at yet another way to the run the JavaScript on her computer. She had already worked on it a lot and she knew that it was really,

really fast. She was trying to unlock one more secret to take her machine from Frankenstein to elite.

Little by little, her mind drifted to thoughts of mermaids, underwater lands of bubbles, crabs, sunken treasures, and friendly conversations with fish and marine mammals. Celia went to the Mermaid Power! gaming site and signed in. As she started to swim around, she saw there were not a lot of people playing at that time. She decided to run a simple test with this computer. She wanted to see if she could get her character to swim faster than it had a few weeks ago, when she'd first stacked the motherboards on her dad's computer.

Celia positioned her small pink mermaid at the beginning of a stretch of ocean that would normally take her about 30 seconds to swim across. She hit the space bar for turbo at the same time as the right arrow key, and she was amazed at what happened next. Two seconds later, when she let up on the space bar, her mermaid had been transported two worlds away. She swam a distance on the game in two seconds that would normally take twenty or thirty minutes to reach. Celia's hand started to twitch in anticipation. Her heart started to race. The computer she built with her family was something truly amazing. The program she wrote by herself to weave together all of the processors and the RAM memory was working better than she had ever dreamed it would.

Celia got up and walked around the house until she found her sister. Anna was in the basement with her headphones on, practicing a song on the electric keyboard. She had a pad on her left side where she was scratching down notes for ideas and lyrics. Her notes were words, pictures, notes in clouds and clusters. She read them back, counter-clockwise.

"Anna, you have to come up to our room, something crazy is happening with the computer."

"What is it, Ceil?"

"Anna, I think we can beat the all-time high score in the Mermaid Power! game. Clear your calendar this Saturday. We are going to have a play-a-thon and try to set the new record."

........
........
........

That Saturday, Celia and Anna both woke up at 6.00a.m. – very unusual for them, especially for Celia. It was a well-known fact she really, really liked to sleep in. They stood half-asleep in the chilly kitchen and fixed themselves toast with peanut butter and honey. They each drank an extra glass of orange juice to give their brains additional thinking power.

Anna looked at her sister. "Are you ready to rock this thing?"

"You know it. Let's go set a new record," said Celia.

They walked down the dark hallway to their room; Celia in her monster slippers and Anna in her pink and white bunny slippers. They walked with the confidence of two people who were about to be the new international high-score champions of a very popular underwater game. It was going to be a good day.

The day did not go anything like what they expected. After the other players realized what was happening, they started trying to work together to keep Anna and Celia's mermaid from racking up more points. The only problem with their blocking tactics was that Anna and Celia had a mermaid that was 10,000 times faster than the rest of the mermaids.

Anna and Celia took turns playing and resting. When they found a difficult puzzle that gave them the opportunity to unlock a new treasure cave, or to upgrade an ability, the sisters worked together to solve the puzzles. Twice, they had to go downstairs to ask Mom or Dad about a question in a puzzle. This was an all-out attempt to break the record and it would take a combined family effort to make their dream come true.

Throughout the day, the score climbed and climbed. By lunch, they were up to 750,000 points, and they had found whole new areas of the mermaid world that no other player had ever visited. They were in a rhythm and they could imagine a path towards the big-time score they were looking for – 1,582,963. The path seemed simple, at least until Rachel Stone woke up in California.

........
........

For Rachel Stone, it was a morning just like any other. She woke up at about 9.00a.m., long after the sun had risen and was shimmering across the water off the Pacific Ocean bay where she lived. She made coffee and read the newspaper headlines on her tablet. One caught her eye: "Cal Tech's President Uses Robots to Fight Pollution". Below the headline, she saw a picture of her former mentor, Dr Elizabeth Washington, smiling in front of a trashcan-shaped silver robot.

Still trying to save the world Elizabeth; I should have known that I could never be your protégé. We are moral opposites, she thought.

Rachel's house was not large above ground; it was built on the edge of a cliff, overlooking the Pacific Ocean. Much of it was carved into the granite of the cliff face, including the bottom of the dolphin tank and her huge computer server vault. She stayed in southern California because she loved to be near the water, even though she did not particularly like to swim. The house where she grew up was less than 150 miles away, but it felt like another world.

After glancing at the headlines, she walked over to her wall of computer monitors and checked how her evil plots where doing that day. She stood there, sipping her coffee, when – WHAM! – she was blasted by three streams of cold saltwater. She turned to see the dolphins nodding their heads excitedly with big smiles. They clicked happily and danced across the top of the water on their shiny green mermaid flippers.

Rachel dried herself in the kitchen and then went to her favorite machine in the far corner of the room to see how things were going in the Mermaid Power! world. As her eyes focused on the screen, she was just taking a sip of coffee. She was so surprised by what she saw, she spit the coffee all over the screen and began to shake with anger.

"Who in the world is threatening to break my all-time incredibly impressive Mermaid Power! score?!?!" she shouted. The dolphins across the room could tell from her voice that she was upset, and they were delighted. They clicked and jumped, saying, "if you are mad Rachel, we are happy".

Her mind was clouded with rage and she began to furiously type on two keyboards at once. She grabbed the mouse with one hand and began to operate a touch screen display with the other. She sorted through maps, showing flashing blue dots for each of the players currently in the Mermaid Power! game, when...

"AH HA!!!," she snarled, "Western Pennsylvania! I remember that house; this is the same person who stumbled into my merworld a couple of months ago!!! AHHH, she has gotten so much better, her mermaid is much faster now. I have to work quickly or my record will be smashed in a few hours!"

Rachel Stone immediately went into what she called her "emergency action plan".

She temporarily paused all of the programs she was running on her collection of computers. She began to send each of the machines into the Mermaid Power! game. She tapped them into the server behind the game and used them to create a swarm of other mermaids. Then she sent all of the new characters to the same place in the Mermaid Power! world.

Inside her house, Rachel commanded a LOT of computing power. As soon as she began to turn her resources towards the workings of the Mermaid Power! game, she began to slow down its servers. Once the serves began to slow, it had the desired impact on the little turbo-charged mermaid with the screen name "C-Ana".

::::::::
::::::::

Across the country in Pennsylvania, Celia and Anna were at the kitchen table, resting their eyes, hands, and brains after their morning of intense underwater mermaid action. Controlling a pink blur as it zipped around the ocean took a lot of focus; it also caused them to work up a big appetite.

As they ate, they did not know what was happening to their little mermaid, C-Ana, as she slowly drifted across the ocean. She was quickly being surrounded by hundreds and hundreds of other players. All of the hundreds of players had been created by computers, controlled by Rachel Stone. They were coming from her wall of master controls at her home on a beautiful cliff in California.

Celia and Anna hungrily ate their lunch of leftover chicken soup and salad. They told their mom about their busy morning collecting golden buried treasures and visiting parts of the map that had never been explored before.

Their mom asked them, "So you are spending your whole day to try and get the highest score ever in this game?"

"Yes, Mom," they answered together.

"Well, what happens then? Do you get a prize or something?"

"No, Mom, no prize."

"And you are only able to get this high score because of the super-fast computer that Celia built, right?"

"Yes, Mom, Celia's computer makes our mermaid go about a thousand times faster than all the other mermaids. She looks like a pink blur of awesomeness compared to all the other slow pokes," responded Anna.

"Well that seems like cheating to me," said Mom. "And I am not raising my kids to be people who cheat." With that, Mom got up and left the table, and the two girls stared at each other. They had not thought of the fact that they were cheating; they thought they were just playing the game much faster than everyone else was.

Well, maybe, deep down, they knew that something was not completely fair about the way they were racking up the points so quickly, but they would not have called it cheating.

Mom did call it cheating, and that word hung heavy on their chests as they walked back into their room to keep playing the game.

When they got back to the desk and looked at the screen, they could not believe what they were looking at.

# CHAPTER 6

There, in the middle of the screen, was their small pink mermaid, just like they expected. However, she was completely surrounded by several thousand other mermaids, all of them purple and all of them with numbers for names:

```
Mer0000001, Mer0000002, Mer0000003
```

All the way up to Mer4627895. Amazingly, as they sat and watched, more and more purple mermaids kept swimming up to join the crowd. In the first minute they sat watching, Mer4627896, Mer4627897 and Mer4627898 all swam up and added their tiny mermaid bodies to the mass of purple on the screen.

Anna was staring in utter disbelief at the screen. She could not understand what was happening.

"What in the world is happening, Celia? It looks like an army of purple mermaids are filling up the ocean! This is crazy! Why did so many people decide to name their characters that crazy name? Why are they all purple? And why have they all decided to join together to keep us from moving?"

In Celia's mind, it was clear. She remembered the JavaScript code she had seen two months before and recognized what was happening.

```
var number = 0;
LoopWhile (number < 100000000000000) {
  //somecode
  number++;
}
```

Every time the function looped, it created another mermaid.

Her mind started to wipe away the fog of all the details that were confusing her.

"This must be the same person. They have access to the back end of the Mermaid Power! server, and they are generating all of these merpeople. They are targeting us. They want to keep us from getting a higher and higher score."

Celia's hands and mind started to move like lightning. She zipped across the keyboard and began to look at the data that was pouring into her own computer. Not only was someone bombarding the Mermaid Power! game with randomly-generated new mermaids, but that same someone was pouring data into her computer to slow its functioning down to a crawl.

It was a lot like what happened two months ago, only this time, Celia knew just what to do. She had been working on a .batch application to trace back the source of attacks. She began to ping the streams of data coming at her computer. She soon realized the attack was coming from California. She started to separate the data and keep it on her hard drive in a special folder so she could look at it later. Beyond that, she just sat back and waited to see what was going to happen next.

After Celia finished her flurry of typing and clicking, she sat back against her chair and took a deep breath. It was then she suddenly realized that Anna was talking to her, saying her name.

"Celia, Celia, hello, what are you doing? What is going on with all of these crazy mermaids filling up the screen? I've been asking you that for 10 minutes and you have been ignoring me."

"Sorry, sis, I didn't hear you at all, my mind wa—"

"What do you mean you didn't hear me? I was five inches away from you, practically shouting your name!"

Celia paused for a second before she spoke. She got that way sometimes, when her own thoughts drowned out whatever was happening around her.

"I'm sorry, Anna, I was concentrating. You know I get like that sometimes."

"Yeah, I know", said Anna. "It's just frustrating to be on my side of it and have no idea what is happening in your sister's brain."

Celia sat up and pointed at the screen. "Here is what's up. See all of these numbers changing right here?" Anna nodded. "That's showing little bits of data coming at our computer. We are being attacked."

Anna looked amazed. "The mermaids are attacking us in REAL LIFE!! That is crazy! I didn't think they were real, I thought they were only on th—"

"No, sis," Celia interrupted, "the mermaids are not attacking us, someone in California is attacking us. It has something to do with the Mermaid Power! site. I would bet you $10 it's the same someone who attacked us two months ago, when we first built that motherboard with the circuits stacked vertically instead of horizontally."

"You mean the time you took the video on the phone of the virus... er... of the code?"

"That's IT!!!! Anna, you are a genius!!!"

Celia shot out of her chair and ran downstairs. Anna was a bit confused but followed a couple of steps behind her.

By the time they found their mom, they were both out of breath. Then they started talking at the same time, saying about a million things at once.

"Whoa, whoa," Mom said, "one at a time."

Celia spoke urgently, "Mom, I need the phone, I need to see the video of the virus again."

"That is perfect," said Mom, "I need you to take that video off of the phone. It is using up all of the memory and I can't take any more videos of Silas doing cute toddler things." Mom walked over to her purse and handed the phone to Celia. "Take the phone, remove the video and bring it right back to me."

"We will," both girls said at the same time.

"I know you will, because I am going up to your room with you to watch you do it." And with that, Mom, Celia, and Anna all walked together towards the girls' bedroom.

Within 10 minutes, all three were huddled around Celia's computer. A cord connected her computer to Mom's phone and Celia was in a screen, carefully moving files to her hard drive. She was a little bit tense because she really needed this process to work.

Just as the last file was in the middle of moving, the phone went blank.

Celia's heart sank. Anna's heart sank. Mom's heart did not sink because she was not looking at the phone; she was watching with amazement at her daughter's supernatural abilities on the computer. But she didn't say anything.

Celia quickly picked up the phone and jiggled the wire. The phone lit back up and the last file finished moving to the computer.

Celia carefully clicked each of the files on the computer to be sure they would all play without the phone. Everything worked the way it should, so Celia unplugged the phone. She deleted the videos from the phone and freed up space again.

"What now?" asked Mom.

"Now we look carefully at the videos and compare the code from two months ago to the code that flooded the Mermaid Power! server today," Celia responded.

"How much code is there to compare?" asked Mom.

"Not much, probably about 1,000 lines in each place, 2,000 lines in total."

"Wait, you are going to compare over 2,000 lines of JavaScript code?" Mom said, with a kind of mystified look in her eyes.

"No way, Mom, that would be crazy. I'm going to write a little program to compare the two batches of code to see if there are similarities. After the program highlights the places where they are similar, I will look at those places with my own eyes. The whole thing won't take longer than an hour to figure out."

Celia's mom looked at her blankly. She did not completely understand what Celia was talking about.

Even though Celia sounded confident, she had no idea how she was going to create a program to compare the two batches of code. She figured she would just start working on it and let the answer reveal itself. The "done in an hour" part was really the only thing she underestimated.

........
........

Celia spent the next three days at school not paying attention. Instead, she was writing out JavaScript code lines in her notebook and thinking about ways to weave the two batches of code together to compare them. The problem was that one was a video and the other was actual text that she got straight from the data.

By the end of each day, she had worked out what she believed to be a reasonable set of code to solve the problem. As soon as she got off the bus, she ran upstairs to try the JavaScript in her notebook. When it did not work, she played around with different parts of the code until dinner.

During dinner, she hardly talked. She just ate, mechanically, while her mind still burned with the problem, thinking, turning over the possibilities. After she finished dinner, she cleared her plate and did her nightly chore from the chore chart. Then she ran back upstairs to finish her homework and try to get in some more coding before it was time to go to sleep.

She did this for three days and three nights in a row. During that time, her mind burned with only the thought of watching the code blend together the two different files, compare them and then generate a list of what was similar between them.

During the three days that Celia was working to compare the JavaScript code, Rachel Stone was on the other side of the country, hatching a new plan to make more money than ever before.

# CHAPTER 7

Rachel was going to test her plan in one of the places she knew best on the internet – BuyGreatJunk.com. Rachel's fourth great love was collecting junk. Or as she preferred to say, she liked to collect "things" or "eclectic items", but most people would call the stuff that she bought from the internet very simply "junk". Not surprisingly, the place on the web where she did most of her shopping also called it junk. In fact, the headline at the top of the website proclaimed, "Been Selling Junk to Folks for Over 20 Years!" The website did not have just a little bit of everything; it had lots and lots of everything.

Were you looking for a giant, inflatable mermaid bouncy house? They had 70 models to choose from. Interested in a fork that fed you so you didn't have to worry about lifting it up to feed yourself? They had seven different styles with six different speeds. It was incredible that a site like it existed, where Rachel could shop until her heart was content; then have it all delivered in two days with their special delivery drones. These auto-piloted drones buzzed right up to her house and dropped off the boxes, packages and envelopes.

Rachel's plan was simple. She knew the site handled millions of transactions each day. Most of these were from people buying stuff. However, many stores sold their merchandise on the site and used BuyGreatJunk's delivery drones to get the products to customers. Rachel also knew from experience that every time someone bought or sold something on the site, along with the amount of money you expected to pay, there were lots of other little fees and taxes associated with each transaction. These fees were how the site made its money. Rachel's plan was to hack into the back-end code that ran the website. Then she would insert a tiny, random amount of money onto each transaction, somewhere between a penny and three pennies. She would then have all of those small transaction proceeds deposited into her various bank accounts in different countries around the world, including the Cayman Islands, the island of Jersey, and Switzerland. These countries were famous for not allowing the police to see into someone's bank account.

By Rachel's calculations, two cents per transaction, multiplied by five million transactions each day, equals $100,000 each day. An average month has thirty days, so $100,000 times thirty equals $3,000,000 for an average month. She would have to pay some fees to transfer the money to the different bank accounts, but even if all of that took 10 percent of her profit, that still left $2.7 million. That is a crazy amount of money. That is enough money to buy 14 houses, or 77 lifted pickup trucks with big mud tires. Rachel already had one giant red pickup truck with tall mud tires, but maybe she could use a few more.

For her plan to work, Rachel had to keep a really low profile. She did what she had only done one other time. She turned off her full-time Mermaid Power! computer so that it would not distract her, or make her angry if she saw someone was about to match her all-time score. For $2.7 million, she could stand to lose her top ranking on the Mermaid Power! site. She could always play her way back to the top spot.

Rachel turned off each of the other evil computer programs she was running. The screens for these computers ran floor to ceiling on the big wall of her main mission control center. Each of the smaller schemes were generating a few hundred dollars a day, and depositing money in various accounts around the world. She was always careful to avoid places where the police could easily look at her money and her account history. However, Rachel didn't want to risk getting caught with any of the smaller schemes while she was working on the evil computer code of her LIFE.

········
········

Back on the other side of the country, in snowy Pennsylvania, Celia continued to work steadily towards her goal. For five days and nights, she tried everything she could think of to solve this puzzle. She consulted books in her school library, she asked questions in online JavaScript coders' forums, and she tried some pretty unorthodox coding techniques.

On day five, she was walking across the playground with Aya, one of her best friends. They were talking about the reading test they had just taken and comparing the answers they gave. It had just rained, and Celia was looking at a little stream of muddy water, flowing across a low spot in the playground. Then it hit her... she knew the answer she had been looking for. She did not even need to write anything down, she just thought to herself, smooth like flowing water.

For the rest of her day at school, she did not think about the JavaScript code anymore. She only thought about and worked on the subjects they were studying in class. The whole way home on the bus, she sat and talked to the people around her for the first time all week. She was relaxed and confident. When she got home, she walked in, hugged her mom and said, "I love you, Mom."

"I love you too, sweetie. Are you going straight up to your room to work on the coding problem?" her mom asked.

"No, I'm going to see what Anna and Silas are doing; I haven't played with them in a few days."

Celia went down to the basement and saw Anna playing on the keyboard while Silas danced, wearing only a diaper and pink sunglasses. Silas was shouting, "Yeah, yeah, yeah, ma, ma, ma, yeah!!!" and he was clapping super-cute toddler claps that were not in rhythm with the song, but for some reason, that did not matter. They were claps of joy, and it made Celia smile to hear and see her little brother having so much fun. Celia started dancing around and jumping up and down with Silas. Anna got so excited watching them that she played her song faster and faster, until she messed up from playing the notes too fast.

After they were all out of breath and Anna's fingers were sore from so much keyboard playing, she asked, "So, did you give up on the comparison code?"

"Not at all, I know I have the right answer now, I just need to rest my mind before I start to work on it. I know it will be the toughest code I've ever created," said Celia.

Then she stood up and started to dance again, by herself, very slowly, in a ballerina way, without any music. Anna and Silas both thought her dance was lovely. They clapped when she was done. Celia gave a little bow.

After Celia finished her dance, her head was clear, she walked up the stairs to her room. She sat down in front of her computer, opened up the JavaScript code editor and began to type. What she typed came easily; it poured out of her through the keyboard into the editor.

Earlier that day on the playground, Celia's breakthrough came when she wasn't thinking about the problem. She was thinking about her reading test and talking to her friend. As they stepped over the little stream of water, she realized what she had been missing. The data in the video file was just like water, it was just little flowing bits of numbers and information.

Celia thought, all I have to do is separate out all the little bits of information and data in the video file, and then it will be a string of text. When my computer was attacked last week, I saved the text that poured directly into my computer as the thousands of purple mermaids crowded the screen during the Mermaid Power! game.

That is exactly what she did; she wrote the code a piece at a time. She had already figured out everything up to the part where she analyzed the video file. Beginning there, she wrote a little code that used a free program from the internet to break the video apart. Then she stored the different pieces as text and compared the text with the data she captured during the last attack. She used a simple program to compare the data and found 500 lines that matched. Printed front and back, they fit on four sheets of paper. The last page finished printing just as Celia's mom called her down for dinner. She folded the paper into thirds and stuck it in the back pocket of her jeans.

·······
·······

That night's dinner was delicious. Mom had made her special tortilla chicken soup, with piles of extra things to add to the bowl to make it exactly how you like it. There were tiny, chopped green onions, little bits of crumbled bacon, shredded cheese, and a container of sour cream to add the final touch right on top of the bowl. Mom also had a plate of warm tortillas in the middle of the table, wrapped in two tea towels to keep them warm. Everyone had a yummy salad at their place, filled with crunchy carrots, sweet spinach and little bits of mushrooms and olives.

Like usual, Silas was the first one at the table. He was wearing only a diaper, even though it was 20 degrees outside. As Mom and Dad brought the food out and set it on the table, he did a little excited up and down dance, clapping and saying, "Yay, yay, yay, mor, mor, mor." He also pointed at himself then pointed at his mouth and laughed with delight.

Mom and Dad had his plastic plate with compartments in the other room for several minutes cooling. They had spread the soup thin across the largest compartment so it would cool faster. As soon as they brought out his plate and set it in front of him, he plunged both hands into the delicious chunks of chicken and beans and began to eat with wild enthusiasm. Soon he was laughing and saying nonsense words, and wiping his soupy hands all over his chest and even into his hair.

Celia and Anna watched Silas eat with amazement.

"Wow Mom, I'm glad you took his clothes off him before you put him at the table," said Anna.

"By the third kid, you learn some lessons," responded Mom. "It's much easier to just let him eat and enjoy himself, with only his diaper, then right after dinner, we can give him a bath and he will be clean and ready for bed."

That night, Celia said the before dinner prayer, and to everyone's amazement, Silas folded his soupy, sticky hands, stopped eating, and whispered little baby words with his head bowed at the same time that Celia said the main prayer out loud. Everyone at the table gave little smiles to each other as they noticed how cute it was that Silas was learning to have the pre-dinner prayer with everyone else.

As everyone ate the delicious food and complimented mom on her cooking, they began to ask each other about their day. When Dad finally asked Celia how her day went, she reached in her back pocket and pulled out the folded paper with the printed code on it. (She had been waiting for that moment.)

Dad took the paper from Celia. "What's this?"

"Oh nothing," Celia said, "just the 500 lines of code that are the same between the attack that hit our computer two months ago and the one that just hit us last week."

"But Celia, that's impossible. That first thing that happened was just a random virus, not an attack," said Mom.

Celia said, "I don't think so, Mom. Computer code is kind of like a fingerprint. Each coder's mind works in a slightly different way. Therefore, each person tends to approach similar problems in a similar way every time they encounter it. Most of these lines are very common bits of code that everyone will use in exactly the same way, but a few of them seem to be unique and are almost like a signature or a fingerprint, showing that these two programs were likely written by the same person."

Celia's mom and dad looked at each other. Then they each looked carefully at the papers and asked Celia about the little bits of code. They underlined in red the parts of it that were especially rare and seemed to be a fingerprint, according to Celia's opinion. The more they all looked at the papers, and the more red lines started to fill up the pages, the more Celia's mom and dad started to get worried.

What happened next was a blur of phone calls and talks with a variety of law enforcement officials.

First, Celia's dad called one of his friends from church, named Larry. He was a detective with the Murrysville Police Department. Within the next hour, Larry was at their house. Then he, Mom, Dad and Anna all gathered around Celia as she sat at her computer and explained each part of the mystery, from the start to where they were now. Celia's grandma had also arrived and was playing trains in the basement with Silas. After looking at all of the evidence, Larry told them this situation was not something for the local police to handle. Larry believed that since this involved cybercrime, they should talk to the FBI. And the next morning, they did just that.

........
........

The next day, Celia did not go to school. Instead, she and her parents went to downtown Pittsburgh. They drove to the Federal Building between Liberty Avenue and Grant Street. In the lobby, they were greeted by a lady in a black suit with a big smile.

"You must be Celia," she said. "My name is Sara Rodriguez; it is very nice to meet you." Sara signed them into a book and they all walked through machines that arched over special red carpets. Celia's mom and dad emptied their pockets and passed through behind Sara.

They followed Sara down a hallway to a collection of eight elevators. She swiped her badge and pressed the button for a high floor. Celia's stomach dropped a little as the elevator flew fast into the Pittsburgh skyline. The elevator stopped and they were in another lobby. They followed Sara down two more hallways and went through several more doors. Each time Sara swiped her badge, a light turned green and she opened a door. She held the door open for Celia, her dad and her mom. As they walked down the long hallways, Sara chatted with Celia about school, what books she was reading, and about her favorite hobbies. Celia was happy to learn that Sara was a professional computer programmer and had even studied computer science at Caltech.

Eventually, they reached a big set of wooden doors. Sara put her hand on a black metal pad beside the door; she put her chin on a chin rest about two feet above the pad. Then she said, "Sara Rodriguez."

Celia was dumbfounded. All at once, she had seen her first palm scanner, her first eye retina scanner, and her first voice recognition scanner. Sara could tell from the look on Celia's face that she was amazed. Sara gave her a little wink and whispered, "I wrote that code."

Just then, the door opened slowly and two security guards met them. They wore plain black suits with blue and red ties. They had on dressy athletic shoes. The taller of the guards bent down and stretched out his large hand to Celia

"Give me five, Celia, it's great to meet you, I'm Tom." He continued, "Mr and Ms Mason, right this way. They are all set up and ready for you folks in conference room one."

Tom led the way down the hall, followed by Sara. Behind her were Celia, her mom, her dad, and in the back was the other guard, Debbie.

The guards escorted them to conference room one. A plain door opened, revealing something truly spectacular. One entire wall of the room was floor to ceiling windows. From the table, you could look out and see the entire city of Pittsburgh, from the football stadium to the Squirrel Hill tunnel, all three rivers, and what looked like two dozen bridges. Celia walked in a daze to the window. She felt a little queasy from being so high. The windows were so clean, she felt as if she could fall right out. She was a little sick to her stomach at first, but she had never seen the city spread out like that. It was truly breathtaking.

When she quit feeling dizzy and got her bearings, she looked around the room. Everyone was staring at her.

"Detective Larry asked you a question, sweetie," Celia's mom said. "Did you hear him?"

"I'm sorry, what? No, I, I was just kind of dizzy from the window. I've never seen a window like this." Celia knew that was kind of a weird thing to say, but it's what came out of her mouth, so she just went with it.

For Celia, the room started to come into focus. There was a long, thick wooden table in the middle with big leather spinnable chairs all around it. In the middle of the table was the computer she had built. Someone had taken it from her room and set it up in here. It was fully set up, right beside another computer, a really nice one. Sara sat at Celia's computer and a man with white hair and a white beard sat at the other computer. Later, she learned that his name is Mr Lee. Along one wall of the room was a long table, loaded with juice and milk in a bowl of ice, a bunch of different kinds of donuts, two large containers of coffee, and a tray with cut-up fruit. Celia's stomach started to grumble and she asked her mom, "May I have some milk and a donut?"

"Sure," her mom answered, "right after you answer Detective Larry's question."

"I'm sorry, what did you ask, Larry?" Celia enquired.

"Celia, I was just telling everyone about how you explained the whole story to me last night with the code, and the attack, and how you built your own computer. And I was just asking you if you could tell everyone where you learned to code JavaScript?"

"Sure," said Celia, as she walked towards the plate of donuts. "I learned from two library books, some online training classes, and by asking some questions on online chat boards. With my mom's permission for the chat boards; she said it was okay for me to participate in them as long as she monitored who was on there and what I was asking."

Sara sat with a big smile on her face in front of Celia's computer. "you mean no one taught you, or showed you any tricks?"

"No," said Celia, as she reached for a chocolate donut with chocolate filling. "No one showed me how to code."

"And how long have you been learning to code?" asked Sara.

"About two months," responded Celia, as she took a seat in a big leather chair. Her dad got her a little bottle of milk and she took a big swig. She looked around the room at all the adults. She had a milk moustache and a little bit of chocolate around the corners of her mouth. The adults had stunned looks on their faces. Everyone except Sara; she just smiled her big, bright smile, looked directly at Celia, and gave her a confident wink.

........
........

In her cliff top command center, things were going well for Rachel Stone and her plan to steal money from the BuyGreatJunk.com website. She successfully broke into the servers that ran the website. Now she was gently probing the different parts of the business, trying to find a smaller corner of the site where a lot of money is transacted, but people are not likely to pay much attention to the finer details of exactly how much they spent.

She was looking for items that were emotional, not financial. At first, she thought about inserting the money-scraping program in the classic car corner. People who bought these cars often felt an emotional attachment to them and because the amounts of money were big, a few cents of additional charges on the final receipt would not be noticed.

Rachel decided against the Buy Great Junk Classic Car Corner. There were two main reasons why. First, since the purchases were so large, there were not that many of them in one day, compared to the rest of the site. Her plan worked by adding a little bit extra to each transaction, so she needed somewhere with lots and lots of transactions, even if they were not very big. Second, some people who traded classic cars did it as a business. They were not emotionally invested at all and did not care about any particular car. To them, the whole thing was about profit. These people were likely to be very careful about the receipts and looked at every item, no matter how small.

Instead, Rachel decided to plant the first bit of evil code in two different sections of the site: the classic toys exchange and the classic album exchange. After a lot of thought, and looking through the ads and sites associated with each of these sections, she decided these customers were the least likely to examine their receipts carefully. They were more likely to be very excited to either play with their new toy or listen to their new vinyl record.

Once Rachel inserted the code in what she thought was the correct place on the servers, she next turned her attention to the customer complaint mailbox. This was the place where customers who had problems with their transactions could send a message to the owners of BuyGreatJunk.com and ask for a resolution.

Rachel assumed that if someone noticed the problem with their bill, they would first send a message to the customer complaint mailbox and ask for the problem to be resolved. Rachel wanted to keep track of the complaints coming in; she wanted to see if anyone noticed her evil plot. She put monitors and filters on all of the complaints coming to the mailbox. Within four seconds of turning on the monitor and filter, she saw her first complaint. Then on average, every four seconds, a new complaint came in. There were less in the middle of the day, and more between 6p.m. and midnight. But they came steadily, and there were a LOT of them. Rachel did some quick math. There are five million transactions each day. There are 86,400 seconds in a day; that means there are about 57.8 transactions PER second on the site. Since the complaints were coming one every four seconds, that means that about one transaction out of every two hundred and thirty-one had a complaint associated with it. As Rachel watched her screens fill up with more and more new complaint messages, she realized there was no way she would be able to monitor them all. BuyGreatJunk.com had hundreds of staff to handle complaints. If she was going to stick with her original intention to try to make mondo money from this plan, she was just going to have to take a chance and hope that she was not caught.

Rachel sat back in her big purple chair and rubbed her hands across the armrests that were shaped like mermaid heads. She tried to clear her mind. What to do, what to do, she thought. She had too many things swirling in her brain. There was only one thing that calmed her down.

Without even thinking about it, she walked over to the special computer with a pink tower case. She plugged the power supply and monitor into a surge protector. She plugged in the internet cord and turned on the computer. Then she went to the Mermaid Power! site, logged in and began to move her little mermaid around the screen.

# CHAPTER 8

**B**ack on the other side of the country, in the tall office building in downtown Pittsburgh, Celia was having the time of her life. She was in a super-secret place, meeting with FBI agents, talking about computers and JavaScript, and all of the grown-ups in the room were listening to HER. This was better than anything she could have dreamed. She had never imagined such a place could exist.

Celia's dad had to leave to go on a work trip to North Carolina. "I love you sweetheart," he said before he left. "Do your best and try to remember everything you can, you are the FBI's best chance to catch this person." A taxi picked him up from the lobby of the Federal Building and drove him to the airport.

For the entire morning, Celia stayed in the conference room with her mom, Sara, Mr Lee, and Detective Larry. While they talked, Sara and Mr Lee projected the same thing that was on their desktop to the front of the room. After about two hours, Sara did something that horrified Celia.

She pulled a small pouch of screwdrivers from her bag, unplugged the computer Celia built, and then she gently turned it on its side. She looked at Celia and said, "I am sorry sweetie, this is going to be hard for you to watch, but I promise I will make it up to you. This really is a beautiful machine, but if you built this one, you can build another."

With that, she unscrewed the case of the computer that Celia had cobbled together. She quickly disassembled the computer and carefully laid each of its pieces on the long table. When laid out side by side, they looked like a piece of abstract art. The space age metallic surfaces contrasted sharply with the dark, organic lines of the wooden table.

Celia sat in disbelief. She remembered the joy she had felt picking out parts from the discarded computers. She recalled how much fun it had been finding something useful and beautiful in the seemingly worthless pile marked "Free". She thought about how hard she had worked with her family the day they cobbled the computer together. How they tried and tried different configurations until finally, when she though there was nothing left to try, they plugged in the power cord and both motherboards lit up. The fans turned on, and they were in business. They had breathed the life of electricity into dead plastic and metal.

Finally, it was too much for her. A tear materialized in the corner of her eye as she watched Sara testing the disassembled components with two wires, a red one and a black one. Celia tried to wipe it away without anyone noticing.

She looked around the room and saw all the grown-ups watching Sara. Celia was doing something important, she was helping the FBI catch a criminal. There was probably no other kid in all of America who was helping the FBI at that moment. She couldn't let these adults see her cry; then they would think they had made a terrible mistake by asking her to help.

Celia quietly got up and got a napkin from the table on the other side of the room. As she walked over there, she whispered to her mom, "I'm going to the bathroom."

Celia's mom caught a glimpse of the shiny dot of a tear in her eye. She heard the slight crack in her voice and the tiniest pause between, "I'm..." and "going".

She knew her daughter was upset, and she knew why. She followed her down the hall to the bathroom and gave her a tight hug once the bathroom door closed and they were safely out of sight.

"Mom, I'm just so sad, I built that computer with my own hands. And they destroyed it."

"I know it is upsetting," her mom said, "but you know there is a good reason Sara is doing that. She seems to know what she is doing, and you are sitting right beside her, so you can just use this as a chance to soak up all the knowledge you can."

Celia sat on a bench in the bathroom and was silent for a minute or two. Her mom went to the sink, wet a paper towel, and came back over, then sat down beside her on the bench and put the damp paper towel on her forehead.

It felt good to have the cool cloth on her forehead. It also felt great to bury her face in her mom's side. She loved the smell of her mom and the feel of her arm around her shoulders. She felt like home, and love, and safety.

After a couple minutes on the bench in silence, Celia rubbed her hands on the tops of her thighs, then brought them down with a loud SLAP.

"Okay, Mom, I'm ready to do this, my country needs me." Celia stood up straight as an arrow and walked with a purpose out of the bathroom towards the conference room. Her mom followed a couple of steps behind.

When they returned to conference room one, there was a different energy in the room. Sara looked at Celia and said,

"Check out what we found buried on the motherboard. The person that attacked you changed the firmware on your motherboard. That is why we took your computer apart, to find something like this. This is the smoking gun."

On the big screen in the conference room, Sara was projecting the picture from a special laptop she had brought into the room. She had the laptop plugged into a slot on the motherboard. On the screen, there was some type of strange programming code. It kept changing and moving, even though there was no power source attached to it.

"How is that code still changing?" asked Celia.

"It is pulling a tiny bit of power from the small batteries that are on the motherboard. It's using that little bit of power to keep itself fresh and to keep looking for additional machines to infect," said Mr Lee.

"Had we not brought your computer into our offices and taken it apart, you would have never found this. No antivirus program would find a virus like this. It is completely unique and very difficult to create."

Just as Celia was starting to get her mind wrapped around what the strange code was doing on the screen, Sara changed the projection again. This time, Celia saw that her hard drive was plugged into the special laptop. Sara seemed somewhat shocked at what she had found.

"Check this out, Celia," she said.

She used the mouse to highlight a small string of random letters in a line of code that somehow Sara had found on Celia's hard drive.

"Do you know what these letters are?" she asked.

"No," said Celia, "but I would love to find out."

"These letters are the backdoor to what is called a Trojan horse," Sara explained. "They are called that because inside of them, they open up to unleash all kinds of crazy stuff into your computer. This is not just any Trojan horse, this is a special one. This one is three layers deep. It is a horse within a horse, within a horse. The person or people we are dealing with are seriously skilled computer programmers and hackers. I'm sure we are going to find a lot more things that were loaded onto your computers."

"Computer-s, as in, plural?" Celia's mom sounded surprised.

"Yes, Ms. Mason, we have a team at your house right now, taking all of the computers, phones, tablets, DVD players, etc. from your house. Whoever was attacking your daughter was out for keeps. I still can't believe all of this started because of an online video game."

"But it is a really fun game," said Celia.

Around lunchtime, four men wearing sunglasses, white polo shirts, and black jackets walked into the conference room without a word. They each held a large duffel bag. They sat the duffel bags against the wall. Once the men left, four more people, each with a laptop like Sara's came into the room. Each person grabbed a duffle bag and parked themselves around the table. Soon the room was filled with the tapping of keyboards, and a million different wires and power cords.

It didn't take Celia long to realize what the people were doing, and that the duffel bags were from her house. They were using the laptops to digitally scrub the family's electronics to see if they had been infected with bad computer code from the mysterious Mermaid Power! attacker.

Two minutes later, Sara got a call from the front desk. She returned with six bags full of sandwiches – cheese steak, capocollo and cheese, and peppers and cheese from Primanti Bros. Even FBI agents need fuel when they are fighting crime. Everyone in the room ate hungrily and used a lot of napkins to wipe all the good juice and cheese from their fingers.

As they ate, Sara came over and sat beside Celia. "Are you okay?" she asked.

"Yeah, I'm fine," Celia responded." I am really having fun watching all of the cool computer gear you get to use."

"Do you understand why I had to destroy the computer you built?" asked Sara.

"You didn't destroy it," said Celia. "The person who attacked it destroyed it by planting all of those viruses. You are just the person who was smart enough to find the viruses and take them apart. You didn't destroy anything."

"Still, I remember the first computer I built with my dad when I was younger... that was such an awesome experience. I still remember the feeling of accomplishment and amazement. I promise when this is all over, I will be sure you get that chance again."

As they sat side by side, eating their sandwiches and chatting about computers, and their favorite simple tricks with computer code, a man wearing headphones and a crazy look on his face busted into the room.

"Sara, Mr Lee, go to the KODA NET. You are not going to believe what is happening."

Sara put down her lunch and ran over to the desktop. She projected the screen onto the large display at the end of the room. She clicked and typed furiously on her keyboard. As the blurs of lines on the screen became clearer and clearer, it was a map. In a short time, Celia could tell it was a map of the United States and Sara was zooming in on Southern California.

After a few clicks, they were looking at a satellite picture of the top of a house in Southern California in La Jolla, near San Diego. The red dot was blinking right on top of the roof of what looked like a nice house on a cliff, overlooking the water.

Sara sat back in her chair and stared at the image being projected on the wall. "Whoever is there is playing on the Mermaid Power! site right now. I can't believe they would get back on there after the attack they launched against you and all of the criminal computer viruses they loaded on your computer. Mr Lee, please see if you can figure out who lives in that house," Sara continued.

The guy with the headphones said, "Oh Sara, it gets better, look at the C3-H data stream. Check out what is coming out of that house."

"Holy cow," said Sara, as she turned the screen over to a big stream of numbers and letters. "Let me turn on the visualization filter." When she did, everything changed. Celia could read that there were thousands of messages about transactions flooding into the house, and thousands of small numbers pouring out of the house. "Something very strange is going on here. I'm going to call the San Diego Bureau office. Folks, grab your go bags, we fly for San Diego in two hours."

In a flash, the room emptied. Everyone had a "go bag" in their office that was filled with exactly the same things; two sets of clothes, $10,000 in cash, in each of three different kinds of money – US dollars, euros for going to Europe, and Japanese yen for traveling in Asia.

Sara looked at Celia and her mom, and said, "Ms Mason, can you and Celia come to California with us? We need Celia's help for my plan to work. I don't know anyone else who can do what your daughter can do."

Celia's mom was very partial to hearing people compliment her daughter. As a reflex she said, "Yes, we will go to California with you."

Within two minutes, Celia and her mom were in a big black SUV, being driven by a professional driver. The vehicle was driving fast. It had two flashing blue lights on top to let the other drivers know this was a law enforcement vehicle on an important mission, and they needed to get out of the way.

During the drive from downtown Pittsburgh to Murrysville, Celia's mom arranged for Grandma Martha and Papa Hil to pick up Anna from the bus stop and to keep watching Silas.

Grandma Martha had already been watching Silas all day. He was helping her plant seeds in her greenhouse.

Celia's dad would be home from his business trip the next day and would be able to pick up Anna and Silas after he got back home.

The black SUV pulled up in front of their house. Celia and her mom jumped out, ran up the stairs, and through the front door. They then ran to their rooms and each quickly packed a bag with two days of clothes, a toothbrush, extra underwear and a swimsuit. They were going to San Diego, after all.

In the blur of packing all the things she needed, Celia noticed that in her room and around the house, there were piles of various size boxes that she did not recognize. She hardly thought anything about it. The last 24 hours had been so crazy; nothing would have surprised her now.

Celia and her mom finished packing at about the same time and ran down the hall, through the living room then out the door and down the steps.

The black SUV drove to the airport with its blue lights flashing the whole way. It normally took 60 minutes to get to the Pittsburgh airport from their house. They made it in 42 minutes.

# CHAPTER 9

Over on the other side of the USA, Rachel was having a lovely morning. She was playing Mermaid Power! and had already found a whole new area of the map she had never seen. Rachel spent the morning trading seashells with different starfish and other merpeople so she could get the wood she needed to start building a shelter in that part of the map. She planned to start a new little settlement there, and use the gold it generated to fund her other main settlement in the center of the map.

She always played the game like that. She would go to an unexplored part of the map, and she would start a new settlement. Then she would build it up over time and use the money and food it generated to make her main settlement stronger. She never sent anything back to the tiny settlements she founded. If they were attacked by underwater monsters, or were destroyed in an earthquake, she just let them go. Rachel did not care. She would rather create a new settlement from nothing than rebuild one that had been destroyed.

As Rachel played, she continued to relax more. On the wall across from her, she had screens flashing numbers and graphs of the money she was making. By that point in the day, she had made $1,248.26. More money was ticking in at about eight and a half cents every second. She also had several screens up, monitoring the complaint messages. By now, she had created filters to vastly reduce the number of complaint messages that made it through to her. She included filters with the words "small fee", "two cents", "unknown charge", "small charge". From time to time, the messages appeared on the screen, but most she ignored. Her programs were set up to divert the most serious ones away from the normal complaint system at BuyGreatJunk.com to her own system.

Rachel would scan the message, look for the amount of money they were owed, and double it, say from four cents to eight cents. Then she would send a check to the person at the address they had written on their complaint message, or the one that was linked to their account. All the checks she wrote came from accounts she had established in the Cayman Islands or the Isle of Jersey. The name on the accounts read "the Buy Great Junk Company" or "A Buy Great Junk Ltd Company". Even though these accounts were not at all connected with the real "BuyGreatJunk.Com" site, when the person receiving the check looked at it, the name was close enough that they would not care.

It wasn't until she started to read these messages that she truly understood how important BuyGreatJunk.com was to some people. It seemed that for some customers, the website was both the only place where they felt safe in the world and their main source of income. So yes, they did look very, very carefully at all of the receipts for the items they bought or sold, and followed up immediately when anything was out of the ordinary.

Once Rachel sent a check to someone, she took their name off the list of accounts that would be randomly targeted for stealing the small amounts of money. She figured that anyone who was diligent enough to check once would probably check every time. She did not need that kind of hassle.

As the day went on, Rachel became more and more comfortable with how her plan was progressing. She was pleased with how she was managing the flow of complaints and the flow of money as it came into her various accounts around the world. Actually, she had a series of collector accounts set up in hundreds of online banks. In those banks, she existed only as a number. They had no proof she was a real person, besides the money that regularly flowed into and out of her accounts.

When any single account collected between $450 and $500, she would automatically transfer that amount to one of her accounts in a different country. This was designed to happen almost randomly, but still within tight controls. She did not want it to be so regular from each account that a pattern was established. She wanted to avoid a pattern because she knew that law enforcement computers and scanning programs looked for patterns. They typically looked for patterns in money coming into or leaving the US, especially if the money was going to certain suspicious places.

Confident that her plan was succeeding, Rachel paid less and less attention to her mermaid and more attention to her accounts and her code that was running on the BuyGreatJunk.com site. She slowly changed the random amount taken per transaction from one cent all the way up to eleven cents. She began to steal from more and more sections of the BuyGreatJunk.com website. She added the audio video site to her code and immediately, she saw a large increase in the income she was generating. She added her code to the classic clothing and children's clothing sections of the site. This addition, paired with the increased income per transaction, brought in a huge increase in the amount of money she was receiving. By the time she got hungry for lunch and left her house to walk to the taco truck down the street, her accounts were receiving about $393 per second.

She bought a delicious fish taco with spicy red sauce and lime. She walked down by the ocean and watched the seagulls fly close to the water then land on the shore and walk along the beach. Her lunch break took about 45 minutes. While she was at lunch, she made about $1 million. (That's enough money to buy four or five houses!)

The day progressed and Rachel began to pull more and more of the small complaints away from the official complaint mailbox at the company. She programmed a steady stream of income to fill up the accounts where the small eight cent to ten cent checks came from.

As the day continued, Rachel began to relax. She went for a run in the park, washed her truck, and went shopping for a new watch. By the time Rachel was ready for bed, she was feeling pretty confident that her plan was going to work. She went to sleep that night around 10.30p.m. By the time she woke up the next morning at 7.48a.m., she had stolen about $12.7 million while she slept. That is enough money to buy 42 houses. This really was an evil plot.

·········
·········

Celia and her mom rode in the back of the big black SUV and they pulled into the backside of the Pittsburgh International Airport on Lindbergh Drive. The SUV rolled slowly up to the gate at the entrance to Defense Avenue, which marked the entrance to the US Defense Department base. The base is located on the land with the Pittsburgh International Airport.

The driver of the SUV slowed at the gate for the guard to check his identification, but the guard did not bother.

"Chuck, you on the move then down'er? Good ta see ya," said the gate guard. Then he pressed the button for their SUV to pass without looking at Chuck's identification.

They drove slowly through the air base. Celia noticed they were surrounded by low buildings. She could see that on the tarmac were a lot of really, really big airplanes with four propellers (two on each wing), and big doors in the back. They were parked at an angle on the side of the runway going away from the city.

Their SUV continued to drive very slowly until it came to the far edge of the tarmac near where a small plane was parked. Two men in uniforms were loading bags into the back cargo compartment of the plane. A tall lady stood straight as an arrow beside Sara, just behind the wing of the aircraft. She wore a black hat and shiny sunglasses, and was resting her hand on the wing as she looked up at the sky, talking and laughing with Sara.

Their SUV stopped. Chuck hopped out of his seat, came around to the back passenger door and opened it for Celia and her mom. He then helped them both out of the vehicle. As they got out of the SUV, he said, "Good luck to yins, I'ope you catch'em criminals. Yins 'an jus walk o'er'ere towards Sara, I'll put your bags on'a plane for yins."

Celia and her mom walked over to Sara, who squatted down so she was eye level with Celia. "Are you ready to do something you will never forget?"

"You know it," said Celia.

They all walked up the little stairs onto the plane. The passengers sat in the back and the lady in the shiny sunglasses sat in the front. As they were all climbing on board, the lady in the sunglasses came over the intercom speakers and announced, "Good afternoon, ladies and gentlemen, I am Captain Kendra Simpson. I will pilot the aircraft today along with First Officer Michael Riedel. Our goal is for you to have a nice, relaxing trip to California. Please sit back, relax and enjoy the flight."

With that, First Officer Riedel grabbed a leather strap on the inside of the staircase door, and he pulled it up hard. The door slammed shut with a click. Once it was in place, he snapped two metal locks on either side of the door to secure it. Then he walked up front to the cockpit with Captain Simpson and strapped into the co-pilot's seat.

Celia was so excited, she could hardly believe what was happening to her. Her first visit to an FBI office. Her first ride in a car being driven by a professional driver. Her first flight on a private airplane in a whole different part of the airport that most people don't get to see or enter. She had no idea what was about to happen next, but she knew it would be memorable.

Once the plane was up in the air, Celia began to look out the window and think about what they were actually about to do. She did not think to bring a game, a book or anything else, so she was pretty bored. It was not a commercial plane; there were no flight attendants offering drinks or food, and there was no entertainment system with a built-in module for movies. Instead, Celia looked out the window and thought, this must have been how my ancestors entertained themselves on plane rides across the country.

Celia's mom sat beside the aisle and she was asleep within three seconds of the plane taking off. It was the longest she had been away from Silas for his entire life. The freedom of not having to take care of him every single minute allowed her to relax and catch up on a little of the two years of sleep deprivation she suffered from.

Celia sat, looking out the window, wishing for something to do. All of a sudden, she felt a tap on her shoulder. She turned around to see Sara with her bright smile. She did not say anything; in fact, she pressed her finger to her lips and gestured her head at Celia's mom to mean, "Shh, she is sleeping." Instead of speaking, Sara gave Celia a book: "The Beginning Guide for Junior FBI Field Agents."

It was a thin book, more like a pamphlet really. As Celia turned the pages and began to read deeper into the instruction manual, she got a clearer picture of just how dangerous and important Sara's job was. She also began to think about how she too might someday make an impact in the world and help other people. These thoughts, along with the excitement she already felt, kept her from sleeping during the flight.

Five hours later, the small plane touched down in San Diego in a slight winter breeze. When Celia and her mom walked off the plane and onto the tarmac of the small landing strip, they were met with a lovely blast of ocean air. They had landed at the US Naval base called Point Loma, and they were just a few feet from the ocean on three sides. To Celia's surprise, the temperature was lovely, not bone-splittingly cold like it was back home. When they left Pittsburgh, it was five degrees, which is twenty-seven degrees below freezing. When they landed, it was fifty-five degrees. Even though that is not warm, it is sixty degrees warmer than Pittsburgh, and it felt wonderful.

The warmth was not the only thing that caught her attention. The smell was amazing; it smelled sweet and a little bit like lilacs. Celia's mom looked at her and said, "Oh wow, smell that jasmine, it must be all around here, it smells like we are in the middle of a big field of it."

Jasmine, thought Celia, what a perfect scent; I need to plant some of this in our backyard next summer. It smells incredible.

Celia and her mom grabbed their little rolling bags from the back of the plane. There were three SUVs waiting to pick up the group. Celia and her mom rode with Sara and Mr Lee in one of the SUVs as one of the local FBI agents drove them to the FBI station's guesthouse and auxiliary command center.

"Hi, I'm Dan, it's great to meet you", the man said as he turned and shook hands with Celia, her mom, and Mr Lee. He had red hair, freckles, and a thick neck. Celia thought to herself that Dan could snap a necktie just by flexing his neck muscles and gritting his teeth. Sara sat up front and chatted with Dan as they wound through the freeways, heading to the Pacific Beach neighborhood.

Celia could hear them talking from her spot in the back seat.

"That's right Sara; she has been in the house since you contacted us. It appears she is still awake and making changes to the code she has installed on the BuyGreatJunk.com site. It is working well; she is on a pace to steal over $33 million each day with that code."

"If only that code were really working," laughed Sara.

"Yeah, seriously", said the other officer, "I don't think she has any idea that she is being set up right now. All the code she wrote and the money she thinks she is stealing is not real."

Celia chimed in from the backseat, "What do you mean it's not real?"

Sara chuckled as she responded, "As soon as we realized what was going on, we contacted the security team at BuyGreatJunk.com. We have been working with them to be sure that from Rachel's perspective, her plan is working perfectly. However, in real life, she is not stealing anything. All the money she thinks she is seeing is not really in her accounts, it is all an illusion. I can't wait to see her face when she realizes it has all been a set up."

"Did you figure out who are the people that are doing all of this?" Celia asked.

"Yes," responded Sara, "the criminal's name is Rachel Stone. She was my classmate at Caltech; I've known her for a long time."

Celia was shocked. "Really?" she asked.

"She and I studied together under the same major professor," Sara continued. "Rachel was a whiz kid. She started at Caltech when she was 16. She did all four years of high school at once, using correspondence courses in different states. The last month of her freshman year of high school, she gave the guidance counselor a stack of straight-A transcripts from thirty classes in four states. She enrolled in the summer program at Caltech two weeks later."

"How did she go from one of the brightest 16 year olds in America to super criminal?" Celia wondered aloud.

"I think those two things do not exclude each other," Sara answered. "In fact, I think it's her incredible mind that tempts her to make money the easy way. She and I both studied under Dr Elizabeth Washington. She is a wonderful woman and a natural born do-gooder; a real save the Earth kind of person. Rachel never understood this and made fun of Dr Washington in private a lot. Rachel called her own way of doing things "lateral thinking". What she meant was thinking of the fastest way to get from point A to point B, ignoring all of the standard social conventions and morals. In fact, Rachel once confessed to me that she did not actually pass all of those high school classes in the same year. She simply hacked into the grading systems from the different states and gave herself straight As. She chose four different states because they were the easiest systems to hack, not because of academics."

Celia pressed on and her mom started to feel awkward about her daughter's tone. "When was the last time you saw Rachel?"

"She was kicked out of Caltech very quietly after she embezzled quite a lot of money with an email scheme. She wrote messages, pretending to be a lawyer in Africa, looking for the heir to a large bank account. The victims of the scheme sent a few hundred dollars to a bank account in Nigeria to process legal paperwork for the bank. Rachel had a system set up where the money was moved from the bank to other locations and then disappeared. Even after Caltech kicked her out of school, the police and the FBI could not prove anything. They never found the money and they could not tie Rachel legally back to the money. By then, Dr Washington and Rachel were hardly speaking to each other, so Rachel did not have anyone to stand up for her to the higher powers in the school. She left Caltech on a sunny Friday morning and I have not heard from her since."

Celia piped up from the back seat, "What is Rachel doing now? What was all of that data coming from her house yesterday?"

Then Sara and the other officer, Dan, told Celia all about the code that Rachel was using to steal money from the BuyGreatJunk.com site.

Celia asked, "What about her plan where she was stealing money from the tax office?"

"Oh, she shut down all of her other code she had going to concentrate on this scheme," Dan said.

"Really?" said Celia. "I wonder why?"

"Hard to say," said Dan, "maybe she didn't want to get caught with a small crime and ruin her chances of a big crime?"

That did not seem right to Celia, but what did she know, she was just a kid and this was her first criminal investigation. She thought she would leave that part up to the grown-ups who worked for the FBI.

Just then, the SUVs pulled up in front of the San Diego FBI station's guesthouse. It was a plain-looking house in the middle of the Pacific Beach neighborhood in San Diego. It was close enough to the ocean that you could smell the unmistakable freshness of the sea. Celia loved that. There were tall palm trees all over the neighborhood that swayed and rustled in the ocean breeze. Celia loved that too.

When she walked in, Celia soon realized that this was not an ordinary house. Everything was set up to look normal from the street, but behind the front rooms were three sets of stairs, leading down several stories.

All of the rooms went basically straight down and out in several directions. Celia guessed the house could comfortably sleep a hundred people if needed. In the middle of each of the underground floors were technology rooms with a lot of computers and big screen projectors like Celia had seen in the conference room in the FBI office in Pittsburgh.

It was very late, but Celia was starving. She was happy to see that someone from the San Diego Bureau office had grilled chicken, ribs, and fresh fish for their visitors from Pittsburgh. They had a pile of warm tortillas on the counter in the kitchen, along with limes, sour cream, avocados, black beans and chopped tomatoes.

All of the visiting agents ate the food hungrily. It all tasted so fresh and delicious. Even the limes did not taste super sour, since they had ripened on the tree in the backyard. As Celia and her mom ate, Celia caught her mom staring at her.

"Celia, I can't believe this is happening. It is totally insane that we are here."

"I know," said Celia, "and I can't wait to see what happens tomorrow."

"It is going to be wild," said her mom. "We better try and get some sleep."

Celia and her mom took their bags to their room. It was down on floor negative 10, which meant that it was 10 stories underground. That is about 100 feet below ground. She and her mom each had their own comfortable queen bed in the same room, with a bathroom attached. Since it was so far underground, there were no windows, no sound, and no light. Once they turned the light off and closed their eyes, they both fell asleep in an instant. Even though they were excited, they were really tired. It had been an intense couple of days.

........
........

The next morning, when Celia woke up, the little bedside clock in their room said 6:42; that meant that it was 9.42a.m. back home in Pittsburgh. By the time that Celia blinked her eyes awake, her mom was already showered, dressed, and ready for the day. She told Celia she was going up to get breakfast, and Celia should pop on up after she took a shower and got dressed.

Twenty minutes later, Celia took the elevator up to the main level. The house was buzzing when she emerged from the elevator. The first thing she noticed was the light. The house was flooded with brightness from all of the skylights. Every room had a skylight and all of the windows were open, letting the crisp ocean air fill her lungs. For a moment, she forgot what was going on and felt as if she were on a vacation at the beach.

The kitchen table was full of fresh fruit from the backyard of the house: oranges, limes, lemons, grapefruit, and avocados. Inside the fridge were three dozen eggs and a pile of Muenster cheese. There were also taco leftovers from the previous night.

Celia was a big fan of having hearty dinner food for breakfast. She had a red snapper taco with cabbage and lime from last night's feast for her breakfast. She also had an entire orange and half an avocado on a toasted, fresh tortilla. Everything tasted so good, she didn't want to stop eating. Finally, when she was so full she felt she was going to burst, she pushed aside her plate.

At that moment, Sara walked in, sipping her coffee from a big red mug. "Good morning, sunshine, you ready to catch your first criminal?"

"Wow, yes I am," said Celia. "Let's do this."

Celia's mom was at the table with her and sat back with a pleased look on her lips. She was ready to see what the day had in store, but she was a little afraid that something bad would happen and that Celia would be in danger.

"Okay," said Sara, "we have been watching the house all night and monitoring the flow of data, both into and out of the house. No one has come or gone and nothing unexpected has happened all night. Fake money from the fake transactions seems to be rolling into Rachel's real accounts all around the world. By crossing so many international borders with her crimes, she is setting herself up for potential prosecution in about seventeen countries on four continents."

"Yeah," piped Dan, "the only place she is safe is Antarctica."

As the day unfolded, little by little, Celia's mom felt more at ease. The FBI had a fleet of cameras already installed all around Rachel's house, and her neighborhood. They also had three drones flying around the area, giving live views of the house and the surrounding area from above.

The little flying planes were pretty amazing, but these were the ones that were like little airplanes. They did not have the drones with mini helicopter rotors that could drop down and look into Rachel's windows. That type was illegal, because of how easy they made it to invade someone's privacy. However, this was frustrating for the FBI because they wanted to see inside Rachel's house and know what was happening in there.

Sara was working to get them access to Rachel's house. She had filed a request to search the house, and she was awaiting approval from a judge. If the request was granted, it was called a search warrant. Judges take search warrants seriously, since the FBI is asking for permission to go into someone's house and look through all their things for proof that they committed a crime. Eventually, the permission for the search warrant came at 10a.m.

Once the news came, all of the FBI agents suited up in what looked like battle gear. They had on thick black vests and combat boots. They all also carried big guns that looked like war guns. They filed out of the house and into the SUVs that had re-appeared on the small street.

Celia and her mom were one floor underground, in the dark room covered with screens. Each of the screens showed black and white video as it came from the various cameras and drones in the area. It was oddly quiet; there was no sound from any of the cameras, only pictures. The only thing that Celia heard was the clicking of keyboards and the slurping of coffee as people drank from their mugs.

Sara and Mr Lee were in the room with Celia and her mom. Sara had on a headset and she was communicating directly with Dan, who was the leader of the search raid. She turned on the communications between her and Dan so that the sound filled the quiet room. They all heard the sound of his breathing, because the mic on the inside of his bulletproof vest was very near to his mouth.

Within a couple of minutes, the three SUVs pulled up to Rachel's house. Celia could see it happening on three different screens at once. Once they pulled up, the SUVs opened and officers poured out in battle gear. Sara switched two of the screens to the officer-mounted cameras the squad leaders had on their helmets. They were now seeing the same point of view that the officers had as they approached the house.

Celia heard Dan announce, "FBI, OPEN UP!!!" She heard a loud bang as they knocked down the door. Then Celia saw blackness in the house and heard a lot of confused sounds. The camera bounced slightly with each step as Dan walked down the hall. She guessed that all of the other FBI agents entered the house and shouted to each other as they looked in each room.

Then BANG, BANG, BANG, BANG. Celia heard Dan scream, "AHHHH!!!!"

"DOWN, DOWN, I'M HIT!" someone shouted in the chaos. The screens in the control room showing the squad leaders' cameras went black.

# CHAPTER 10

Celia heard Dan shout, "AHHHH, GLITTER!!!! There is some kind of trigger that covered us all in super sticky liquid, maybe glue, and pounds and pounds of silver, purple, and pink glitter."

"Glitter??" said Sara. "That is definitely the same Rachel Stone I remember, always playing tricks on people."

"Glitter," said Mr Lee.

"Ahhhh, glitter!!!" said Celia. Then it all made sense to Celia. She knew Rachel was long gone.

One of the other agents came to Dan's camera and wiped it with the thumb of her glove so that the agents in the control room could see the inside of the house.

"Sara," Celia pleaded, "Rachel is not in the house, she is headed out of the country. You need to turn your team around and have them look towards the border with Mexico."

"Celia, what are you talking about?" asked Sara.

"It's the M.M.M.," said Celia, "the Mysterious Mermaid Manifestation."

"The what?" asked Sara.

Celia continued, "In Mermaid Power!, the M.M.M. is the fastest, best, most powerful way to escape a huge, bad situation where there is no other way out. A master player might only use it once a year, only when they are in a desperate situation."

"Like when your house is about to be raided by the FBI," said Sara.

"Exactly," Celia replied.

········
········

The FBI teams did not leave Rachel's house. They went ahead and served the warrant on the house and searched it for evidence. They found Rachel's pet "mermaids" that were happy to see people other than Rachel, even if all the officers were dressed like robots, wearing their black battle gear.

They entered her large command room and it was filled with smoke and the smell of burning metal parts. The agents put on gas masks just in case. They found her wall of monitors, and her pink Mermaid Power! computer. In a corner, in front of the wall of windows overlooking the ocean was her comfy chair with the mermaid armrests. As the agents continued to search, they found there were not a lot of belongings there. The closet in the bedroom did not have many clothes. The refrigerator was empty, except for some French fizzy water and part of a salad in a restaurant takeaway container. The cabinets in the kitchen only had one cup, a small plate and a bowl.

The FBI agents carried two dozen computers and various other mechanical devices out of the house, but they did not need to bother. All of the computers had been wiped clean. The same mechanism that triggered the glue and glitter upstairs had sent thousands of self-destruct signals to all of the computers. This had completely destroyed the motherboards and set fire to the hard drives. The machines the agents confiscated were still smoking and smoldering, and they might as well have been bricks. They were no longer functioning computers.

Once the agents certified that the house was safe, Sara allowed Celia and her mom to go to the house with her. They drove a short distance and arrived at the location in a couple of minutes. As they walked around, they got a strange feeling. Something was missing. What were they missing?

The volunteers from the Southern California Sea Mammal Sanctuary arrived and lifted the dolphins out of their tank. The dolphins began to lose their minds, moving their heads and clicking. Bertha, the strongest dolphin, escaped from the volunteers and crawled on the floor to the kitchen. She hit the door to the utility closet with her nose. As the volunteers struggled to lift her, one of them opened the closet by backing into the door. Once the door was ajar, Bertha nudged the fake wall of shelves over and over. Just before the volunteers carried her away, she managed to knock the fake wall of shelves loose and it opened up, revealing a hidden tunnel.

"What in the world?" said the volunteer. He called over one of the agents to show her what Bertha had found.

"This is crazy," Sara said. "Well, at least I don't feel so bad about allowing her to escape; she has had this planned for a long time."

"But how did she know that we knew?" Celia asked.

"Rachel is one of the most intelligent people in the world," responded Sarah. "She must have seen something that let her know we were on to her."

"But what?" asked Celia.

........
........

To find the answer, we need to rewind to the day before...

Just about the time that Celia, her mom, and Sara were getting on the plane in Pittsburgh, Rachel was realizing that something was wrong. It was too easy to steal money from BuyGreatJunk.com, something did not feel right.

Everything she did in the BuyGreatJunk.com system worked. It was like they had removed all of the security around everything she touched. They know I'm in here, thought Rachel.

To test her theory, she raised her per transaction amounts to super-high levels. She finally reached the levels of $.185 to $.262 per transaction. When the money kept flowing in, she knew she had been discovered. She was certain a raid on her house would come next, she just didn't know when.

At 10.30p.m., she got up from her computer and went up to her room. She took a shower and put on comfortable clothes. She grabbed a light rain jacket and her purse, which contained her passports and US $50,000 (more than enough money to buy two new cars). She had no phone. She walked downstairs through her huge planning room, past the dolphin tank and into the adjoining kitchen. She stepped into the utility closet and shut the door behind her. She slid back a fake wall of shelves and it revealed the entrance to a small tunnel. She hopped up into the tunnel and the shelves snapped back in place behind her. It was as if she had never been there.

She crawled through the tunnel for two-and-a-half hours. She had it constructed shortly after she bought the house, for an occasion just like this. She reached the end of the tunnel just before 1a.m. She popped her head out from the manhole cover in the sidewalk on La Jolla Boulevard, near the corner with Westbourne Street. She waited at the bus stop for five minutes and then hopped on the number thirty bus, taking it to the Gaslamp Quarter neighborhood. She reached the Gaslamp Quarter at 2a.m. She walked into the lobby of the elegant hotel on corner of West Harbor Drive and Pacific Highway.

Rachel wore sunglasses, even though it was night, and carried a designer handbag. This disguise helped her fit right in with the nicely-dressed clientele of the hotel. No one thought twice about her sitting in the lobby for several hours, sipping coffee and reading the pages of The Economist newspaper. Because she occasionally looked at her watch, they assumed she was waiting on someone.

At 4.30a.m., she walked out of the hotel lobby, waited at the corner for 10 minutes, and caught the express bus to Tijuana,

Mexico. The ride took 30 minutes. After 20 minutes, they crossed through the US/Mexico border. A US border patrol agent boarded the bus, looked at everyone's passports, going from seat to seat, and greeted each passenger in English or Spanish, as he thought appropriate.

When he reached Rachel's seat, he said, "Buenos Dias."

"Good morning, officer," Rachel responded. She removed her passport from her purse and handed it to the officer.

He looked at it, handed it back to her and said, "Have a great day in Mexico."

With that, Rachel Stone became an international fugitive who had successfully fled the United States.

Rachel reached the central bus station in Tijuana at 5a.m. She enjoyed a delicious breakfast from a vendor with a cart outside the station. She chose a fried donut, covered in cinnamon and sugar, called a churro. This came with a hot cup of fresh cocoa. As she dipped each bite of the churro in the hot cocoa, it soaked up a bit of the chocolate and made the cinnamon and sugar come alive in her mouth. The smell of the breakfast reminded her why she loved Mexico, and why she was happy to be back.

Rachel bought a first-class ticket on the next express bus to Guadalajara, Mexico, in the center of the country. The ticket cost $2,330 Mexican pesos, which is about $138 U.S. dollars. She also bought the seat beside her for an additional $2,330 pesos, just so that no one would sit beside her and ask her questions. In the gift shop of the bus station, she bought a travel pillow, earplugs, a little blanket, and two bottles of water.

The bus ride took 11 hours, but since she had a first-class ticket, her seat folded all the way back so that it was flat like a bed. After she boarded the bus, she chatted for a few moments with the people around her. She opened one of her waters, took a big drink and then set both bottles in the empty seat beside her. She got out the travel pillow and blanket, inserted her earplugs and reclined her seat all the way back. She was asleep within 10 minutes of the bus getting on the road to Guadalajara. Rachel slept all the way there with her arms around her handbag.

........
........

Back in San Diego, at the FBI station house, the mood was not as jovial as it had been the night before. The agents from Pittsburgh were all trying to recreate what went wrong. Some were on laptops, others were in the operations room downstairs, in front of the large monitors. Several still had a lot of gold, purple, and pink glitter in their hair from Rachel's house.

Celia felt completely crushed, and it showed on her face.

Sara walked up to Celia and her mom. "How are you two doing?"

"How did we miss her?" asked Celia. "She slipped right through our fingers."

"That's funny," said Sara, "our FBI bosses in DC are asking us the same question. All I can say is that it isn't over. We are pretty sure she is in Mexico, and we have great cooperation with the Mexican police on cases like this. Rachel is in all of the international databases. There is no way Rachel Stone will be allowed to leave Mexico and go to any other country."

"It just seems so wrong," said Celia. "She was right there." Celia pointed at one of the screens, which still showed a camera shot of Rachel's deserted house, on the cliff looking out on the Pacific Ocean.

"Being a success is not about having everything go perfectly all the time," said Sara. "It is about learning from your mistakes and getting better. That is what we are going to do here, get better."

........
........

Rachel arrived in Guadalajara after 11 hours of sleep, feeling refreshed but starving. Instead of getting something to eat, she took a taxi directly to Guadalajara International Airport. She arrived at the airport at 8.30p.m. She walked up to the ticket counter and asked for a first-class ticket on the 11p.m. flight to Havana, Cuba. The ticket agent charged her $1,300 for the ticket and scanned her passport, which said her name was Elizabeth Castillo.

"Everything is set for an on time departure, Ms Castillo. Will you be checking bags with us this evening?"

"No," said Rachel, "I'm traveling light; it's just a quick trip to visit my family."

Rachel casually walked through the security line with her first-class ticket. She was treated respectfully by the Mexican guards, who were screening passengers as they passed through to the boarding area.

While waiting for her flight, Rachel devoured a freshly-made Torta de Milanesa, which is a specialty in Guadalajara. It is a sandwich with freshly-baked bread, lots of lettuce, tomatoes, ripe avocado, and a thin piece of pork chop that has been coated in breadcrumbs and fried.

Once she had eaten her dinner, Rachel looked around at the boutique shops in the international departure area of the airport. She found a lovely purple and silver dress that fit her perfectly, and some stylish, comfortable shoes to match. She walked into the dressing room, tried them on, and paid for them at the register of the boutique with US dollars in cash. Since she was not using a credit card, Rachel knew it would be impossible for the FBI in America to track her.

After she bought the lovely, new clothes, she gave her old clothes to the lady at the checkout line and asked her to take care of them. The lady at the register took them, folded them, and stashed them under the register. She thought they were nice. She would take them home, wash them and give them to her daughter.

········
········

It was 9.30p.m. Pacific coast time in San Diego, and Celia's heart was still broken. She was folding up her clothes and preparing to go home the next day with her mom on a commercial flight back to Pittsburgh. They would not be flying back in an FBI plane, since there was not an urgent need for them to get anywhere as soon as possible. All the excitement and hope that had carried Celia when they came to San Diego felt long gone, even though it had only been 24 hours since they arrived.

Celia just kept turning over in her mind who was this Rachel Stone and where had she gone?

········
········

At exactly that moment, Rachel Stone was walking through the passport check at the Mexican customs, preparing to leave Mexico and board a plane to Havana, Cuba.

She handed the Mexican customs agent her Mexican passport. As she left the country, cameras in the visa line captured images of her face. These images instantly flew across the internet to the Mexican Federal Police servers, and ran across the algorithms, checking each person's facial proportions against known criminals in an international database. Rachel's photo instantly lit up a hit in the US Consular Consolidated Database of US photos taken for visas and passports.

Her face flashed across the desk of an analyst at FBI headquarters in Washington DC, who compared her photos from the Guadalajara Airport with her known passport pictures from her official US passport. The analyst typed "confirmed" into the box on her screen. This told the system that she had looked at both sets of photos and thought that the person leaving Mexico really was the same person who the FBI was looking for from the crimes in San Diego.

........
........

Sara Rodriguez and Dan immediately received calls on their cell phones. They ran outside the FBI station house, jumped in a car, and were on their way to the airport two minutes after they received the call. Within an hour, they were in a small plane, flying to Havana, Cuba.

........
........

Rachel boarded her flight at 10.30p.m. and enjoyed the three-hour journey in the first-class cabin. She watched a movie, read a magazine, and thought about how nice it would be to enjoy the warm sun and beaches in Havana this time of year.

As she walked off the plane in Havana, she did not notice Sara and Dan. They just seemed like two more of the hundreds of people on flights arriving in Havana on that sunny December day.

Sara immediately recognized Rachel and led Dan in her direction.

This does not look like someone who is an international fugitive and has stolen tens of millions of dollars around the world, Sara thought. I guess you cannot tell what someone is capable of just by looking at them.

As Rachel walked through the airport, she slowly began to feel that she was being followed. Within a couple of minutes, there were four Cuban police officers surrounding her. Sara and Dan were immediately behind her. She turned and looked at Sara.

"Sara?" Rachel said with surprise.

"Hi Rachel, long time no see. Sorry we have to meet like this." Then Sara repeated the script she had to say. "Rachel Stone, we are with the FBI, you are under arrest."

"But you can't do this, I'm in a foreign country, I'm in Cuba. The US does not have an extradition treaty with Cuba. The Cubans won't send me back to America to be prosecuted," said Rachel, as the Cuban authorities were putting handcuffs on her.

"Sorry," said Sara, "things are changing quickly between the US and Cuba; we just signed a two-way extradition treaty. They don't want our criminals and we don't want theirs. Bad luck for you, it was just signed last week; you really should keep up with these things."

With that, Sara and Dan, and the four Cuban officers walked Rachel out to the FBI plane, and put her on board.

Within 40 minutes, they were all on their way to Washington DC to put Rachel Stone in jail, where she belonged.

··········
··········

The next morning, Celia and her mom woke up early and took a taxi to the airport. Celia did not see Sara before she left San Diego and that made her even sadder. She could not believe how all of this had gone so badly.

When they arrived at the airport and checked in for their flight, Celia's mom could tell that she was feeling pretty down.

"Tell ya what, how about we go to the bookstore and I will buy you any book you want for the flight back to Pittsburgh?" said Mom.

"Ooookaaaay," droned Celia. Normally, there was nothing Celia liked better than going to a bookstore, especially an airport bookstore. But this morning, everything just seemed so completely gray and hopeless; she couldn't get excited about anything.

Celia walked into the bookstore and made her way towards the science books. As she did, she passed a stand with newspapers. From the corner of her eye, she thought she saw two familiar faces. She walked backwards two steps and took a good look.

On the front page was a photo of Sara and Dan, with a short lady standing between them. There she was, Rachel Stone, looking confused as she stepped off the plane early this morning near Washington, DC. The headline read, "First successful extradition from Cuba in 60 years!"

Celia kept looking and she realized that each of the major papers had the same story on the front. Celia's mom bought one of each and read them all the way home.

"Mom, I can't believe that after all, that is how they caught her."

"I can," said Mom. "It is poetic justice. After she used computers and software coding to steal money from so many people, it was a computer system that matched her face and caught her. Even a fake passport and traveling to two foreign countries didn't let her sneak past the law enforcement databases."

They both laughed, and gave each other a big hug.

........
........

Six hours later, they were back at their house in Murrysville, Pennsylvania. The FBI had paid for a professional maid service to come and clean the house from top to bottom, wash all the dirty clothes, cook two meals and leave the food in the refrigerator. They did that to make up for confiscating and destroying all of their electronic devices.

The FBI also replaced all of the electronic devices with new ones: cameras, cell phones, the television, etc. In Celia's room, where her hand-made computer had been on her desk, it instead held a stack of books and a catalog filled with computer parts. On top of the presents was this note:

"Celia,

I'm so glad our paths have crossed. You are awesome and we never could have solved this case without you. Check out these books with other languages: JAVA, .Net, C, ADA, Python, Groovy – now you'll be able use the best language for each type of program you want to create. Let me know when you have questions, I'm happy to help.

Order anything you want in the computer parts catalog – use this account number: 984736. Let me know when all your hardware arrives. I will come over and help you build your next amazing machine.

We will work together again soon, I am sure.

Your friend,

Sara"

Celia flipped through the stack of programming books; she would start to devour them tomorrow. For now, she returned to her love of new hardware. She grabbed her pen, the parts catalog and her flashlight, and climbed into her bed. She made a tent with her blanket, snuggled inside, and started slowly turning the pages. Within minutes, her mind was imagining ways to fit the computer pieces together in strange ways. Some things never change.

# FREE DOWNLOAD

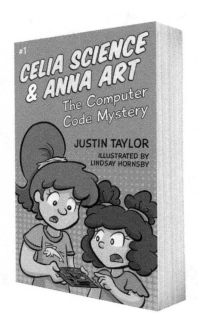

Sign up for the author's New Releases mailing list and to download a FREE copy of this audio book.

Click here to get started:
www.celiascience.com/book1

# ACKNOWLEDGEMENTS

Thank you to all the people who make the Celia Science and Anna Art Series happen. My amazing wife, Carolyn, you are the love of my life. My daughters, you are the best beta-readers and story development wizards in the world. My editor Heather Cole, developmental editor Meg Lawson (http://ebooksandcooks.com). Help with techie details of this story: Javier Sevilla, Ronald (Buck) Babich, Greg DiPietro. Fantastic illustrations: Lindsay Hornsby (http://lindsayhornsby.com/). Beautiful cover design and layout by Leila Dewji and her team (https://iamselfpublishing.com). General marketing help, inspiration, coaching - Nicole Holland (http://bbrshow.com/) and the TC crew! Fantastic audio book editing by Dawn Tee. Audio book music: Alonzo Pennington. Shout out to my audio book sponsors- Twin Engine Coffee! I love your business and I LOVE your product! (http://twinenginecoffee.com/) Huge shout out to the launch team for this book! I love you all and you are amazing!!!

Most importantly thank YOU reader! You ROCK and I'm so thankful you took the time to read this book! Send me a message and let me know what you think: (http://celiascience.com/) or Justin@celiascience.com

# ABOUT THE AUTHOR

Justin Taylor is a writer, science enthusiast, amateur artist, husband, insatiable book reader, dancer, crepe maker, and father. He was born and raised near Cayce, Kentucky. He currently lives near Pittsburgh, Pennsylvania and writes books about how the Mason kids use science, art, and creativity to solve mysteries. When he was a kid, he loved the Encyclopedia Brown Series and still keeps a few stashed around his house for emergencies.

http://celiascience.com/about/

CPSIA information can be obtained
at www.ICGtesting.com
Printed in the USA
LVHW111751301020
670290LV00004B/560

9 781911 079170